Quinn needed to know the truth, and she needed to know her sister was safe.

"Everything okay in here?" a man said, the voice so unexpected Quinn jumped.

Malone stood on the threshold, his broad shoulders nearly filling the space.

"You scared a year off my life

"Sorry," he said easily.

"It wouldn't matter if I hadn't already had ten years scared off back in the woods."

He nodded, his expression hard. "Things could have gone really bad back there."

"I know. If you and my brother hadn't come along, they would have gotten Jubilee."

"And killed you." The words were so blunt, his voice gruff.

"They didn't."

"When did you notice them following you?"

When had she?

She remembered spotting the truck on her way through New York, seeing it again a few hours later in Pennsylvania. "They were following me for a couple hundred miles."

"Seems odd that they were able to pick up your trail so far from home."

She hadn't thought about that. She'd been too busy trying to figure out how to escape them.

Aside from her faith and her family, there's not much **Shirlee McCoy** enjoys more than a good book! When she's not teaching or chauffeuring her five kids, she can usually be found plotting her next Love Inspired Suspense story or wandering around the beautiful Inland Northwest in search of inspiration. Shirlee loves to hear from readers. If you have time, drop her a line at shirlee@shirleemccoy.com.

Visit the Author Profile page at Harlequin.com for more titles.

MYSTERY CHILD

SHIRLEE McCOY

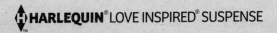

⟨H⟩ HARLEQUIN® LOVE INSPIRED® SUSPENSE

If you purchased this book without a cover you should be aware
that this book is stolen property. It was reported as "unsold and
destroyed" to the publisher, and neither the author nor the
publisher has received any payment for this "stripped book."

Recycling programs
for this product may
not exist in your area.

LOVE INSPIRED BOOKS

ISBN-13: 978-0-373-67756-6

Mystery Child

Copyright © 2016 by Shirlee McCoy

All rights reserved. Except for use in any review, the reproduction
or utilization of this work in whole or in part in any form by any
electronic, mechanical or other means, now known or hereinafter
invented, including xerography, photocopying and recording, or in
any information storage or retrieval system, is forbidden without
the written permission of the editorial office, Love Inspired Books,
195 Broadway, New York, NY 10007 U.S.A.

This is a work of fiction. Names, characters, places and incidents are
either the product of the author's imagination or are used fictitiously, and
any resemblance to actual persons, living or dead, business establishments,
events or locales is entirely coincidental.

This edition published by arrangement with Love Inspired Books.

® and TM are trademarks of Love Inspired Books, used under license.
Trademarks indicated with ® are registered in the United States Patent
and Trademark Office, the Canadian Intellectual Property Office and in
other countries.

www.Harlequin.com

Printed in U.S.A.

I know that I will live to see the Lord's goodness
in this present life. Trust in the Lord. Have faith,
do not despair. Trust in the Lord.
—*Psalms* 27:13-14

To my ever faithful God.
Who sees me in my weakest state and loves me anyway.

ONE

They were coming.

She could hear them as clearly as she could hear her pulse pounding frantically in her ears. Feet crunching on dry leaves, clothing brushing against pine boughs, the sounds of pursuit ringing through the dark forest.

A twig snapped, and Quinn Robertson shrank deeper into the tree throw, her arms tight around her five-year-old niece. Jubilee didn't speak, didn't whimper or cry or beg for her mother. She hadn't made a sound since they'd left Maine twelve hours ago.

Please, God, don't let her make one now.

The prayer bubbled up, borne of desperation and just the tiniest bit of hope that it would be heard.

Please...

A light bounced over the thick tangle of roots that jutted up from the hole Quinn cowered in and swept toward the ridge she'd just run down.

Tumbled down. She'd been terrified, and she hadn't been careful. She was *still* terrified.

Had her brother, August, gotten her message?

Did he know how close she was to his house?

Did he realize she should already have arrived?

If she'd snagged her purse before she'd taken off, she could have texted to let him know she was in trouble, but she'd left it in the Jeep, her cell phone inside of it. There hadn't been time to grab anything but Jubilee. By the time her niece was out of her booster seat, the car that had been following them, the car Quinn had pulled off the road to avoid, had made a U-turn and was heading back in their direction.

She'd run into the forest that lined the rutted country road. She'd had no other choice. Tabitha had entrusted Jubilee into her care. She'd begged Quinn to bring the little girl to her father in DC. Her *real* father. Not the man Tabitha was married to—the man who'd left bruises on Jubilee's cheek, bruises on Tabitha's throat. The one Quinn had known nothing about. She hadn't known her sister was married. She'd had no idea Tabitha had a child. Five years had passed since she'd seen her sister face-to-face, and suddenly she was at Quinn's door begging for help, her eye black, finger-sized bruises trailing down the column of her throat.

Quinn hadn't hesitated. She'd agreed to do what Tabitha was asking. She probably would have agreed even if her sister had told her how much danger she might find herself in.

A lot of danger. More than she should be facing alone.

Quinn shuddered, holding her breath as someone raced past her hiding space. Jubilee lifted her head from Quinn's shoulder, her long braids snagging on roots that jutted into the tree hole.

Please, don't cry, Quinn wanted to say, but a light slid over their hiding spot, illuminating the darkness for a heartbeat of time.

Quinn eased deeper into the hole, the loamy scent of earth mixing with decaying leaves and rotting wood. Branches jabbed into her ribs and back, scraping skin off her shoulder as she pressed into the root system of the fallen tree.

A voice called out. Someone answered, footsteps pounding on the ground nearby. The hunters weren't giving up. They were determined to find their prey.

Did they realize how close they were?

Could they hear the frantic pounding of Quinn's heart? The quiet panting of Jubilee's breath?

How long would it take for them to discover the fallen tree? The hole Quinn and Jubilee were cowering in? Long enough for August to find the Jeep? If he was out looking, if he'd gotten her message, if he realized she and Jubilee were in trouble, he could be there in minutes, but that was way too many "ifs" for Quinn's peace of mind.

Leaves crackled, branches broke and Quinn could hear the loud gasping breaths of someone just feet away. She tensed, her arms tight around Jubilee. She had to protect her. She'd promised Tabitha that she would. Of course, at the time, she hadn't realized she was putting herself at risk. Knowing the truth wouldn't have changed anything. Quinn still would have agreed to Tabitha's plan. Only she would have been much better prepared.

Instead, she'd blindly believed a sister she hadn't seen in years and headed out with no weapon, no plan for protecting herself or Jubilee.

It will be easier to disappear if we're separated. Take her to DC. Her biological father is there. Don't call the police or contact anyone before you get there. My husband has money, and he knows people who would be happy to help him get me back. If Jarrod has to use Jubilee to do it, he will. The best thing for her, and for me, is for you to get her to DC. The kid deserves better than what she's been getting. I guess maybe I do, too.

The kid…

Such a strange thing to call your own child. It should have been a clue that something wasn't right, that maybe Tabitha wasn't being completely honest.

Too late to worry about that now.

Quinn had to find a way out of the mess she was in. She scooted backward, the soft rustle of leaves making her freeze.

"Over here!" a man yelled, and Quinn bit back a scream.

She expected the roots that hid them from view to be pulled away, for a monster in the guise of a person to suddenly appear.

Jubilee's arm snaked around Quinn's neck, her fingers tangling in Quinn's hair. The five-year-old was terrified, her body shaking, but she didn't make a sound.

Good girl, Quinn wanted to say, but leaves crunched and twigs snapped, and she knew their pursuers were closing in. Two men? Three? She hadn't gotten a good look. She'd been too busy sprinting through the trees.

Please, God, don't let them find us.

Please.

The prayer whispered through her mind, a knee-jerk reaction to hard-core terror. She'd prayed like that before. The day after Cory's brain cancer diagnosis, the weeks during his radiation and chemo treatments and at the end, when there'd been no hope, when Cory had been nothing but a shell of the man she'd married, she'd begged and pleaded and petitioned God.

Maybe He'd heard.

Maybe He hadn't.

He hadn't answered. Not in any way that had mattered.

Light splashed across the fallen oak, highlighting the giant tangle of roots that she and Jubilee had crawled beneath. She forced herself to stay still as the light found its way to the other side of the oak. The night went dark again, the woods silent and still. Leaves fell through the cracks in the root system, dirt raining down on Quinn's head as someone moved past. Probably so close he could have reached in and grabbed Jubilee from Quinn's arms.

She was stiff with fear, numb with it. She wanted to run and find another place to hide, but she didn't know where the guy with the light had gone. There were no more shouts, no more pounding footsteps. Just the darkness, the silence and Jubilee's arm around her neck.

In the distance, a car engine broke the silence, the sound growing closer with every passing second.

August?

If he'd gotten her message, he'd be out looking for her. She knew that. Just like she knew him. August was quick to plan and to act. He never hesitated. Not when it came to the people he loved.

That's why she'd called him when she'd first realized she might be being followed. It's why she'd listened when he'd told her to drive to his rural Maryland property. He'd promised to contact Jubilee's father, have the guy meet them at August's place.

It makes more sense than you driving to DC alone, Quinn, he'd said. *If Tabitha is lying, you could be in a boatload of trouble for taking that kid out of Maine. The sooner you get her in her father's hands, the better.*

Not something she hadn't thought about, but thinking about it hadn't been enough to make her break the promise she'd made.

In for a penny. In for a pound.

That's what Grandma Ruth had always said. No sense beginning something and not finishing it. At least not in her mind, and not in Quinn's.

The car rumbled closer, the forest remaining silent. Not an animal moved, not a leaf rustled. The stillness terrified Quinn, the thought of someone lurking just out of sight made her pulse race. Jubilee shifted, the fabric of her dress swishing, the noise overly loud in the silence.

"Shhhh," Quinn wanted to warn, but she didn't dare make a sound. The car engine died, a door slammed and a long low whistle broke the silence. Somewhere in the distance, a man called out, his voice edged with panic. Feet pounded on dry leaves, branches snapped. Someone was running, and he wasn't being quiet about it.

Was he calling off the hunt for Quinn and Jubilee?

Please, God...

Just that. She had nothing else, no profound prayer to offer, no bottomless well of hope. She'd used up every bit of faith she had when Cory was sick. Now, she planned for the worst, worked toward the best. She'd spent the past few years rebuilding her life, repaying medical bills that had piled up so high she hadn't been sure she'd ever see the end of them. She'd worked full-time as a kindergarten teacher, part-time as a janitor. Sixty, seventy, eighty-hour workweeks, going home to the tiny efficiency apartment over Martha Graham's bakery. She'd lived off ramen noodles and peanut-butter sandwiches. Two months ago, she'd finally paid the last medical bill. Now she was building her savings, looking down the road to a time when she could purchase a little house a few blocks away from Echo Lake.

If she survived tonight.

If a dozen things that could go wrong didn't.

Another car door slammed, the sound reverberating through the forest. Tires squealed and an engine roared. Then, the world went silent again.

Quinn waited until her legs were numb, her arms stiff, before she moved. She waited until a night owl called from a nearby branch and a small animal scurried through the tree's exposed roots. Finally, she eased out into the cool night air, Jubilee still clinging to her neck.

Moonlight filtered through the thick tree canopy, dappling the leaves with gold. She glanced up the ridge she'd barreled down. Her Jeep wasn't far from the top, parked in the small clearing she'd veered into when she'd realized the black SUV she'd spotted on the interstate had followed her onto the narrow road that led to August's house. She could walk back to the Jeep, but she didn't trust that the men who'd been following her were gone. Sure, she'd heard a vehicle drive away, but she'd also heard one arrive. Maybe it had been August, or maybe it had been someone else. Someone who wanted to get his hands on Jubilee?

Quinn couldn't take chances with the little girl's life.

She'd have to walk through the woods until she reached August's property. She hefted

Jubilee onto her hip, pried the little girl's fingers from her neck.

"Just a little looser, sweetheart," she murmured. "If I pass out from lack of oxygen, we'll both be in trouble."

Jubilee didn't respond, but her gaze darted from Quinn to the ridge.

Her silent watchfulness wasn't normal five-year-old behavior. Quinn worked with kids every day, had been teaching for years, knew exactly how most children Jubilee's age would act. Typical five-year-olds didn't stay quiet during long road trips. They didn't stay quiet when they were scared or hurt, either. Of course, this wasn't a typical situation. Quinn couldn't really expect Jubilee to act in a typical way. Maybe she would start talking once she was reunited with her father. *Daniel Boone Anderson.* The name was scrawled across the sealed manila envelope that Tabitha had thrust into Quinn's hands. Beneath that, an address and phone number had been printed neatly next to the word *HEART*. Jubilee's father. His work address and phone number.

That's all Tabitha had said about the envelope.

The envelope that Quinn had promised not to open. The one she'd left tucked under the driver's-side floor mat in the Jeep.

A soft sound drifted through the darkness.

Not leaves crackling or twigs snapping. Just a whisper of something that shouldn't be there. A shifting in the air, a soft sigh.

Quinn froze, her arms tightening around Jubilee as she scanned the darkness. Nothing but shadowy trees and bushes, but the night had gone quiet again.

Was someone moving along the ridge? A dark figure darting through the trees?

She turned and barreled into a hard chest.

She screamed, the sound ripping from her throat as she tried to run. Someone snagged her shirt, dragged her back. She screamed again, Jubilee's terrified howls mixing with hers.

A hard hand slapped over her mouth.

"Shhhhh!" a man hissed, but there was no way she planned to go quietly. She slammed her head into his chest, tried to knock him off balance. If she could loosen his grip, she and Jubilee might have a chance to escape.

Having a head shoved into his solar plexus wasn't exactly how Malone Henderson had planned to spend the first morning of his vacation. A couple of eggs, buttered toast, some canoeing on Deep Creek Lake—that had been the plan.

A wiggling, squirming, head-butting woman was not.

Neither was a screaming kid.

He pulled the woman up against his chest, tightening his grip just enough to keep her from slamming her head into his chest again.

"Enough," he said. "You want whoever ran you off the road to find us?"

The woman mumbled something against his palm. The kid shrieked even louder.

This was definitely not what he'd had in mind when he'd left HEART headquarters the previous day, fought his way through Beltway traffic and headed to the tiny vacation rental that he'd planned to spend seven very quiet days and nights enjoying.

"With how loudly the kid is screaming," he said, hoping that reason would win out over terror and that Quinn Robertson would calm down enough to calm down the kid, "your brother isn't going to need me to call in our location. He'll find his way here all on his own. So will whoever else happens to be hanging out in these woods."

Quinn stilled, all the fight seeping out of her.

The kid was another story. She sounded like one of the baby hogs Malone's grandfather had kept on their Tennessee farm, squealing frantically for her mother.

Only Quinn wasn't this kid's mother.

If Malone's boss Chance Miller was right,

August McConnell's other sister, Tabitha, wasn't the little girl's mother, either. Her mother was Boone Anderson's deceased wife. Boone was the kid's father, and five years of searching, five years of hoping and praying that the infant Boone's wife had stolen away from him would be returned, had finally ended. Boone would have what he'd been praying for. He'd have his child back. Everyone at HEART was focused on making sure that nothing went wrong, that the little girl who might be Boone's would arrive in DC safely.

If Boone hadn't been on the way home from a hostage rescue mission in Turkey, he'd have been the one hanging onto Quinn Robertson listening to the kid scream. Boone had been notified of his daughter's supposed return. He'd be stateside in thirty hours. Until he returned, Malone and Chance were taking responsibility for the child. There'd be lots of questions, lots of police and FBI involvement.

And Malone was going to be in the middle of it all until Chance arrived from DC. Another two hours maybe. That's what Chance had said when he'd called to ask Malone to drive to August McConnell's place. It had seemed like an easy enough thing to do. Malone was taking his vacation in a cabin not too far from McConnell's property. All he had to do was wait around until Chance arrived.

Of course, things were never as easy as they were supposed to be. At least not in Malone's experience.

And, this?

It was proving to be pretty complicated.

He eased his hand from Quinn's mouth, took a step away. He hadn't meant to scare her or the child. He'd been working out of an abundance of caution, making sure that the person crawling out from the roots of an old tree wasn't armed and dangerous. He and August had found Quinn's abandoned Jeep, they'd heard men moving through the forest, they'd assumed trouble. Doing that was a whole lot better than winding up dead.

"No more screaming, kid," he said quietly.

"Telling her that isn't going to make her stop," Quinn muttered, taking a step back and then another. If she kept going, she'd fall into the hole he'd watched her climb out of.

"And running from me isn't going to keep you safe," he responded, snagging her elbow as her foot slipped between thick roots. The tree throw had been a good hiding place. He'd give her that, but she should have stayed put until her brother arrived, and she knew she was safe.

"Watch it," he cautioned, pulling her away

from the roots. "We don't want to end our first meeting on a bad note."

"We sure began it on a bad note. Where's August?" she asked, shrugging away, her arms still tight around the little girl.

"Probably hiding until the kid stops shrieking."

"She wouldn't be screaming, if you hadn't terrified her." There was no heat in her words, no fear. For someone who'd been run off the road and chased through the woods, she seemed calm.

"I know, and I'm sorry. I wasn't sure who was coming up out of that hole, and I didn't want to be shot before I figured it out."

She nodded, her attention on the girl. "It's okay, Jubilee. Everything is going to be fine."

She smoothed thick braids that fell over the kid's shoulders.

Red braids?

It was too dark to see, but Boone's little girl had red hair. At least, she had when she was a baby. Malone had seen the photo in Boone's office, sitting right next to the one of his new wife and their children.

"Hush," Quinn murmured against the girl's hair, and to Malone's surprise, the kid pressed her lips together and stopped screaming, the abrupt silence thick and heavy.

He glanced around, eyeing the shadowy trees and the heavy undergrowth. Anyone could be hiding there, and all it would take was one bullet to take Quinn or the little girl out. If that was the perp's goal. If not, Malone would be the target. Take him out. Grab the kid. Get out before August arrived.

"Let's go." He took Quinn's arm, leading her toward the ridge and the Jeep that was parked at the top of it.

"August—"

"Is smart enough to figure out that we're not going to wait out in the open for him to show," he cut her off, digging into his coat pocket and pulling out the little pack of chocolate candies he always kept there. Years ago, he'd used them to bribe his siblings and cousins. Now, he used them to comfort scared kids. A necessity, because he wasn't like Boone or Chance or Chance's brother Jackson. He didn't have the ability to look kind or easygoing or harmless. Most kids took one look at Malone's face and were terrified. According to his coworker Stella Silverstone, that wasn't because of his scar. It was because of his scowl. One he apparently wore all the time. The candy might not make that any easier on the eyes, but it sure helped get cooperation from kids. That went a long way

when he was trying to get them out of dangerous situations.

"You hungry, Kendal?" he asked, holding the
little packet out to her.

"Her name is Jubilee," Quinn said.

"Not if she's Boone Anderson's daughter, it
isn't," he responded, smiling as the kid took the
candy from his hand.

"Even if she's his daughter, her name is Jubilee. That's what she goes by. It's what she
knows. Forcing her to respond to something else
would just be cruel."

"Okay. Jubilee it is." It wasn't his battle to
fight, and he wasn't concerned one way or another with the kid's name. What he was concerned about was getting her to Boone alive.

That shouldn't have been a problem.

Chance had assured him that the job would
be easy. Meet August McConnell at his house,
wait with Quinn Robertson and the little girl
she was traveling with until Chance arrived.
Go back to his vacation.

Piece of cake.

Only, of course, it wasn't.

That was a lot worse for Jubilee than it was
for Malone. He could vacation anytime. He had
plenty of leave saved and plenty of freedom to
go when and where he wanted. Jubilee deserved
better than this, though. He planned to make

sure she got it. He'd spent too many years helping raise his four siblings and six cousins to
want to spend much time with kids now, but
he wasn't going to let a child be hurt or scared
without doing something about it.

Maybe that's why he loved his job so much.
He got to effect change in the lives of kids like
Jubilee all the time. As a matter of fact, half the
cases he'd worked for HEART involved kids
who were being used, abused or held hostage.
It seemed as though that was the way of the
world—the innocent were often the most ill-
used.

God was still in control, that's what Granddad
Cooper had always said. Granddad had been a
preacher. He'd also been caregiver to a houseful
of kids. All of them left orphaned when their
parents died in a multivehicle car wreck outside
of Reedville, Tennessee. That wreck had cost
Granddad Cooper his two oldest sons and their
wives, but it hadn't cost him his faith. He'd held
fast to that through the next twenty-some years
of trying to raise eleven kids.

Malone probably could have learned a thing
or two from that. If he'd ever slowed down
enough to think about it.

He frowned, eyeing the top of the ridge.

The silence was bothering him. A lot. So was
the fact that August hadn't shown up. With all

the screaming Jubilee had done, Malone would have expected a guy like August to come running. He had *ex-marine* written all over him— quiet, gruff and not too keen on strangers showing up in the darkest hours of the morning. Not surprising. Chance had done a background check before he'd called Malone. According to him, August had served in the Marine Corps until three years ago. He'd taken a medical discharge, then, and had worked private security ever since.

Malone had spent forty minutes with the guy, and he could say for certain that August didn't do patience, he didn't believe in waiting and he'd never hold back when he could be taking action.

Unless something kept him from doing it.

Or someone.

Malone didn't believe in leaving anyone behind, but he couldn't risk Quinn and Jubilee's lives. He'd bring them back to August's place. Once he made sure they were secure there, he'd return for August.

What he wouldn't do was the expected.

Quinn's Jeep and August's vehicle were at the top of the ridge. If someone wanted to stage an ambush, that would be the place to do it.

"Change of plans," he said, taking Jubilee

from Quinn's arms. "We're going to walk to your brother's place."

"I can carry her." Quinn reached for Jubilee.

"That will slow us down."

"I ran through the woods with her in my arms. I think I can manage a short hike."

"You can, but is it the safest option?"

"What's that supposed to mean?"

"Jubilee was screaming like a banshee, and your brother didn't show up. That could be because he was a good distance away and wasn't sure what direction the screams were coming from, or it could be because someone stopped him." He didn't hold back, didn't have time to soften his answer.

"That's not a pleasant thought."

"No. It's not. Neither is the thought of you carrying Jubilee if some guy comes charging after us. She's little but so are you, and it will be a lot easier for me to run with her than for you to."

"I prefer *petite* to *little*," Quinn muttered, moving beside him as he followed the ridgeline. She took two strides for every one of his, her small frame drowning in an oversize sweatshirt.

"If you're dead," he responded bluntly, "I guess that won't matter."

She didn't respond.

He guessed she'd gotten the point.

Stella would have had a field day reaming him out for his less-than-delicate approach. Fortunately, she wasn't there. Something was going on, and until Malone knew what it was, he didn't have time to waste playing nice.

He jogged through the trees, the kid's long braids slapping his shoulders and face. She had a bruise on her cheek. He could see the dark smudge of it against her pale skin. He thought there were freckles on her nose, too.

Freckles and red hair?

He didn't ask Quinn. No talking. As little noise as possible. Every cell in his body focused on getting them out of the woods and to safety.

Up ahead, a shadow moved through the trees. Silent, barely visible in the darkness. Malone reached for Quinn's hand, yanked her behind a huge evergreen.

"What—?"

He pressed his finger to her lips, gestured for her to be quiet. For a moment, he heard nothing. Then, furtive steps. The hunter on the prowl. He handed Jubilee to Quinn, pressed them both deeper into the pine needles.

"Stay here until I come back for you," he whispered in Quinn's ear, the words more breath than sound.

She nodded her understanding, and then he slid back into the forest, heading for the shadowy figure that was stalking them.

TWO

Quinn had never liked horror movies. Right at the moment, she felt as if she were living in one. Only this wasn't a movie. This was real-life terror. This was her alone in the woods with an innocent life depending on her. She didn't know where the guy had gone. She didn't even know what his name was. All she knew was that he'd told her to stay put until he returned.

From where?

That's what she needed to know.

Had he seen something?

Heard something?

How long should she wait?

Ten minutes?

Twenty?

Jubilee's head rested on her shoulder, her hand lax against Quinn's bicep. She was exhausted, of course. Probably terrified, too. She'd been left with a stranger, carted hundreds of miles away from her home, and now she was

in the dark woods waiting for something horrible to happen.

Quinn wanted to ease out from behind the
tree and creep through the woods until she
found her brother's house. She was afraid,
though, terrified of making a mistake. If Cory
were here, he'd know what to do. A deputy sheriff in Echo Lake, he'd always known exactly
what every situation required. He *wasn't* there,
though, and Quinn would have to figure this
out on her own.

Somewhere beyond the tree, leaves crackled.
She waited, expecting to hear men's voices, a
shouted warning. Fist against flesh. Something.
Anything.

She heard nothing but that soft crackling
sound.

She edged back until she was wedged between pine boughs, the sharp, tangy scent of
broken needles filling her nose. Jubilee had
gone still, one hand clutching the little bag of
chocolate candy she'd been given, the other
clutching a fistful of Quinn's jacket.

She still hadn't spoken, but those screams?
They'd probably stay with Quinn for the rest
of her life. They'd been the sound of profound
terror. No child should ever have to feel that.
She shifted her grip on Jubilee, listening for

any sign that August's friend was returning. Friend? Maybe. Quinn had no idea who the guy really was. He hadn't introduced himself, and she hadn't thought to ask how he knew her brother. She hadn't gotten a good look at his face, either. She had noticed the scar that bisected his cheek, though. If she'd met him before, she'd have remembered that.

Jubilee shoved against her arms, trying to wiggle down. Quinn held tight. No way was she putting the child down, but August's friend had been right about one thing—running with a five-year-old in her arms wasn't going to be easy. Quinn had her mother Alison's build—small-boned, short, thin. Her sprint from the Jeep had been fed by adrenaline. Now, she felt tired, her arms aching, her legs trembling. Still, she wanted to run. She just wasn't sure what direction to go.

They couldn't stay there forever.

Eventually, the night would pass, day would dawn, and they'd be sitting ducks, waiting to be spotted by whoever was after them.

Tabitha's husband?

It was the only thing that made sense. Quinn had no enemies. She barely had any friends. Funny how people pulled away during times of grief. Strange how those that she'd been closest to seemed to have drifted the furthest after Cory was buried. Or maybe *she'd* been the one to drift away, separating herself out from the pack of happy, successful couples that she and Cory had once gone bowling with, camped with, biked and hiked with.

She shook the memories away, ducked beneath the pine boughs and stepped out of the shadow of the tree. She had to move or she'd be frozen forever, too terrified to do anything but wait for someone to find her.

Jubilee stared at her through eyes made dark by fatigue. Wisps of hair had escaped the braids they'd been plaited into. A few long strands straggled across her neck and curled up to touch the bruise on her cheek.

Poor kid. She hadn't slept much during the long drive. She'd just sat in her booster, staring out the window. She hadn't spoken, but she'd responded to questions with nods or shakes of her head. Obviously, she had a good receptive vocabulary. There was no doubt that she'd understood everything Tabitha had said to Quinn. She knew she was going to DC to see her biological father. Had she met Daniel Boone Anderson before? That was something Quinn should have asked, but she'd been too shocked by Tabitha's sudden appearance to think straight.

A light flashed to the right. There. Gone.

Someone searching through the woods, and whoever it was had probably heard Quinn shuffling through the dead pine needles and fallen leaves.

Quinn didn't dare stop, didn't dare go back to the tree or duck into another hole. They'd find her this time. She was certain of it.

She sprinted into a thicket, brambles and branches tearing at her hair and snagging the comfortable yoga pants she'd worn for the ride.

She barely felt it.

Keep going. That's all she could think about. *Run as fast as you can.*

Jubilee's weight slowed Quinn down, but she pushed through the other side of the thicket, dodging through trees. Her foot caught on roots that snaked out of the ground, and she fell hard, skidding on her knees, one hand on the ground, the other clutching Jubilee.

A man stepped out in front of her, appearing so quickly, she thought she must be imagining the dark form.

He moved toward her and she scrambled up.

"I have a gun," she lied, her voice shaking.

"No, you don't. You're a pacifist to the core," the man responded, his voice so familiar, she wanted to cry with relief.

"August?"

"Yeah, and you're lucky it is. Didn't Malone tell you to stay hidden?" he responded.

"Not exactly," she hedged.

"Exactly," a man said, his voice coming from behind Quinn. "I told you to stay put until I got back."

"I decided I'd be safer heading to my brother's place."

"Your brother was the one I saw walking through the trees. If you'd given me half a minute to check things out, you could have saved us all some time."

"I gave you more than half a minute."

"Learn a little patience. It might save your life one day," he retorted, his eyes blazing through the darkness.

"How about we discuss this at my place?" August cut in. "I'll feel a whole lot better about everything once we're not standing in the woods making it easy for any sniper who happens to be skulking around."

A sniper?

That wasn't something Quinn wanted to think about.

She shuddered, clutching Jubilee a little tighter.

"I agree," Malone said. "I don't know about you, McConnell, but I'm not liking the way things are playing out."

"You want to walk or go back to my SUV?" August asked. The fact that he was asking surprised Quinn. August had been doing his own thing and going his own way for as long as she could remember. He'd joined the marines at eighteen, been discharged honorably five years later. Now he worked private security, traveling around the country doing work for a high-profile security firm. He didn't ask anyone for advice, and he never seemed to need help.

"It's your call. You know the area better than I do," the guy responded. Malone? That's what August had called him. Maybe they were old military buddies. Quinn would have to ask. After they got out of the woods.

"Let's walk to my place. I'll come back for the SUV after law enforcement gets here."

"You called the police?" Quinn had promised Tabitha that she wouldn't. She'd kept that promise the same way she'd kept so many others. She was big on that. Keeping promises. Mostly because her father had never kept his. Not to her mother. Not to her. Not to any of his children, friends or relatives.

Danner McConnell had been a conman. A liar. Sometimes even a thief. He'd been charming, too. Funny. Always at every dance recital or school performance. He'd liked people, and people had liked him, but he'd never made a promise he hadn't broken. He'd never sacrificed anything for his family. He'd died of a massive heart attack Quinn's senior year of high school. She'd been sad, and she'd been relieved. For the first time in nearly three decades, Quinn's mother had been free to live her life happily. No husband scheming and jostling to get whatever he could from whomever he could. No explanations needed for money borrowed and never repaid, tools taken and not returned. The jovial, sweet guy who'd mowed the lawn for the neighbor and cheered from every audience was what Quinn tried to remember, but in the back of her mind, she couldn't quite forget all the promises broken and all the nights she'd heard her mom crying in her room.

"I called the police when I found your Jeep. The door was open, the keys were in the ignition and you were gone. The police seemed like a good idea," August replied as they walked back the way Quinn had just come. Apparently, she hadn't been sprinting toward his house. Who knew where she and Jubilee would have ended up if August and Malone hadn't stopped them.

"I guess they were, but Tabitha—"

"Is just like our father was. You know it. I know it. She's a liar, a thief, a con woman."

"Was those things. People change."

"Some people change," he grumbled. "Our sister isn't one of them."

"Jubilee is her daughter," Quinn retorted. "How about you have a little respect for that?"

To his credit, August didn't say another word about Tabitha. "Sometimes we have to break promises to keep our word, Quinn," he said instead. "You're going to have to tell the police everything she told you."

"I can't do that. Tabitha said—"

"A promise isn't a good one to keep if it gets you killed," Malone broke in, lifting Jubilee from her arms. "Whatever she said, whatever she told you, doesn't matter in light of the fact that you've been followed here. The more the police know, the easier it will be for them to figure out what's going on."

He was right. She knew it, so she kept her mouth shut, and trudged behind August, Malone right beside her. Jubilee seemed comfortable enough in his arms, her head resting against his chest, the candy still clutched in her hand.

She'd felt heavy, but Quinn knew she was small for her age. Probably an inch shorter than the smallest kid in Quinn's kindergarten class. Someone had painted her fingernails pink with tiny flowers in the middle of each nail. She had a pretty diamond and gold necklace that Quinn thought was the real deal, a beautiful coat that had probably been purchased at some fancy designer shop, patent leather shoes, and the look of a child who had been given just about anything and everything she wanted.

Except for the bruise.

That was the one discordant note in an otherwise perfect picture, and it made Quinn's heart ache. To have everything you wanted and nothing that mattered? That was the cruelest irony of all.

The faint sound of sirens drifted from somewhere in the distance, the local police responding to August's call.

Or the state police?

Either way, the promise Quinn had made Tabitha had been broken. There was no way to undo that, and Quinn didn't know if she'd have wanted to. Despite what she'd said to August, she knew Tabitha had looked her square in the eye and lied.

There's nothing to worry about, Quinn. You're not breaking any laws, and my husband couldn't care less about Jubilee. Not his kid. Not his concern. It's me that he wants. Plus, he's got no idea that I came here. Vegas is far away, and he doesn't know I have a sister in Maine.

Maybe not, but he'd figured it out, and Quinn was sure her sister had known he would. Tabitha had been edgy and anxious when she'd stood on Quinn's doorstep. She'd refused to go inside, refused coffee, tea, food. She'd kissed Jubilee once, told her to be the best girl she could and taken off before Quinn could ask questions.

It had all happened fast, and Quinn knew that was purposeful, knew that her sister was protecting herself more than she was protecting her daughter. She had to have understood just how easily her husband could find her and Jubilee. She should have warned Quinn. She should have told her to be prepared for anything. Instead, she'd smoothed things out, made them nicer than they were.

Just like August had said—she was like their father.

Her daughter could have died because of it.

Her daughter…

Malone had called Jubilee by a different name. Kaitlyn? Kendal?

Quinn had been too terrified to really listen to what he was saying. She needed to ask more questions, she needed to get some answers. First, though, she needed to get to August's house and away from whoever might still be lurking in the woods.

They made quick time, heading east on a path August led them to. It wouldn't take long to get back to the ranch-style house that stood in the middle of acres of corn fields and pastures. That was good, because Malone didn't like the feeling he was getting. Trouble. It seemed to pulse around them, mixing with the howling of sirens and the soft rustle of leaves and pad of feet.

"Where'd you tell the police to meet us?" he asked. "If they're at the Jeep, you might want to call and let them know we're heading toward your place."

"I gave them my address. They'll be there when we arrive."

"Do you think they'll take Ju…" Quinn's voice trailed off. She must have realized it wasn't a good question to ask in front of the five-year-old. The kid had already been through a lot. She'd been thrust into the arms a stranger, driven from Maine to Maryland. Everything she'd known, everyone who was familiar, was gone.

She didn't cry, though. Didn't complain. Didn't ask for Quinn, her mother or her father. She just rested her head against Malone's chest, the bag of candy he'd given her hanging from her hand.

Odd. Maybe even a little alarming. Most of the kids he brought out of traumatic situations wanted the familiar, begged for whomever it was they were closest to. This kid didn't seem as if she wanted anyone or anything. Except, maybe, to be left alone.

If she really was Boone's daughter, he'd have his work cut out for him. Building a bond with a child who didn't seem to have bonded with anyone wasn't going to be easy.

Then again, maybe she had bonded. Maybe she was in shock or so terrified she was afraid to speak.

He patted her narrow shoulder.

"It's going to be okay, kid," he said, and she looked square in his eyes. For just a second, just enough time to make his pulse jump, he saw Boone in her face. Something about the tilt of her eyes, the freckles that were definitely on her nose. It was enough to make him want to put her in his SUV and drive her straight to HEART headquarters, keep her safe there until Boone arrived.

He couldn't. Not without getting into a boatload of trouble with the local PD and with Chance. Malone's boss liked to play by the rules. He liked to do things by the book. He did not like to get on the bad side of law enforcement.

They trekked up a small hill, pushing through thick foliage. Despite her short stature, Quinn kept up, her pale face and panting breaths the only sign that she was wearing down.

"You doing okay?" he asked, and she nodded.

"Dandy," she panted, the response almost making him smile.

"I hope you feel that way when we get to the house," August grumbled. "You could go to jail, sis. You could be charged with kidnapping. You know that, right?"

"I didn't kidnap Jubilee. Tabitha asked me to bring her to her father."

"Tabitha. Right." The disgust in August's voice was obvious.

Malone didn't question it.

He didn't want any part in family drama.

He'd had enough of that to last a lifetime. He loved his siblings and his cousins, and he hadn't minded helping to raise them, but he'd done his time, and now he enjoyed the freedom that came with being single.

Most of the time he enjoyed it.

Lately, he'd been a little tired of returning to his empty apartment, sitting up late at night, dozens of memories filling his head. He had his demons. A man couldn't do the kind of work Malone did without them. Some days, he wished that he had someone to fight them with.

That was the truth.

One he didn't like to admit even to himself.

"Tabitha really has changed," Quinn whispered as if somehow that would keep Jubilee from hearing.

August snorted.

"She has!"

"We'll see if you still feel that way when you're sitting at the local sheriff's office explaining why you've transported a missing child across state lines."

"What are you talking about, August? I did what her mother asked me to do."

"If this little girl is Daniel Boone Anderson's daughter, then Tabitha is not her mother. I've done a little research while I was waiting. Anderson's daughter was kidnapped by his former wife."

Jubilee stiffened, her muscles going taut, her little hands pushing against Malone's chest. She might not be saying a word, but she understood everything they were talking about, and it was upsetting her.

"That's enough, McConnell," Malone said quietly. He didn't want to scare the little girl more than she'd already been.

August didn't get the hint. He just kept talking. "Nothing to say to that, sis? You've always been quick to defend people. Even people who don't deserve it. Tabitha is not just a thief and a liar. She's a kidn—"

"I said," Malone cut in, "that's enough."

"Not nearly," August replied.

"How about you stop thinking about your vendetta against your sister long enough to consider the kid's feelings?" Malone growled.

That shut August up.

Up ahead, blue-and-white lights flashed through the trees, the tinny sound of a police radio drifting on the chilly night air.

"Looks like they're there," August said. "I'll run ahead and fill them in."

He sprinted forward, and Quinn muttered something Malone couldn't hear.

"What's that?" he asked, glancing in her direction. Strobe lights splashed across her face. There were scrapes on her neck and on her cheeks. Probably from hiding in the tree throw and running through the woods.

"Nothing I want to repeat in front of Jubilee." She took the little girl from his arms, hugged her tight. "Everything is going to be okay, sweetie. I know it will be."

She couldn't know it. Not with any certainty. Life played out the way it did. God did what He would. All they could really do was trust that He had things in control.

Malone didn't correct her.

There wasn't any sense in that.

Besides, Jubilee deserved a little comfort before she got handed over to more strangers.

And then to Boone?

Malone hoped so. That was the goal. Get her back to her biological father.

If she was Boone's kid.

One way or another, the police would figure things out. Before they did, they'd probably hand Jubilee over to Child Protective Services. Which was a shame, because Boone wouldn't be in-country for another… Malone glanced at his watch…twenty-nine and a half hours. He'd want to see the girl as soon as he arrived. That might be difficult if CPS secreted her away.

Still…

If she was Boone's kid?

That would be something.

Everyone who worked for HEART knew how long and hard Boone had hunted for his daughter. She'd disappeared while he'd been overseas, serving his country. His first wife had joined a cult and taken their newborn baby with her. By the time Boone returned to the States, everything he'd thought he'd had was gone—his wife, kid, money. All of it had gone to the cult.

He'd hired a lawyer, petitioned for custody, but his wife had gone so deep into the cult it had been difficult to find her. She'd died of a drug overdose a few months later, their daughter taken by members of the cult. Despite the efforts of police and FBI, she'd never been found.

Eventually the case had gone cold, but Boone hadn't given up. Even after he'd married again, he'd kept looking.

If this was his daughter, all those years of believing she'd eventually be found, all those years of following dead-end leads, tracking down friends of friends of his deceased wife, would pay off. All that hope that Boone had held out, all the belief and faith he'd poured into the search? It would be worth it.

That would be nice to see.

Malone considered himself a cynic, a little rough-edged and definitely more logical than emotional, but even he liked a good story and a happy ending.

If Jubilee was Boone's little girl, that would be the kind of happy ending everyone at HEART worked for. A coup for the entire team; and something that would be celebrated by everyone.

If…

The story Quinn had told her brother didn't jive with what Malone knew. According to Quinn, the five-year-old had been living with a real estate broker named Jarrod Williams. If he had any ties to the cult Boone's first wife had joined, Chance hadn't been able to find it.

A little more time would bring everything to light. It usually did. For now, they had to keep track of Jubilee, make certain that she didn't disappear again, and convince the police that she really could be Boone's child.

He glanced at Quinn again, her small frame drowning in the oversize sweatshirt, her hair just brushing its collar. If she hadn't called her brother, if she hadn't told him when to expect her, she might still be hiding from the men who'd followed her from Maine.

Or worse.

She might be dead.

They'd have to make sure she stayed safe, too.

They?

He was on vacation.

As soon as Chance showed up, he was going back to it.

Until he showed up, though, Malone would stick around. He always completed his missions. This time would be no different. He just hoped that finishing it didn't mean sticking around for days or weeks. That seemed to be the way things went—he agreed to help for a few hours and ended up helping for a lot longer.

He pushed through a thick stand of trees, stepping off the path and into a small field that butted up against a wide well-manicured yard. The small ranch house August lived in was just ahead, the glow of the porch light faded beneath the onslaught of emergency lights. Three police cars were parked in the driveway, and two officers stood on the porch, talking to August.

"Looks like this is it," Quinn said so quietly he almost didn't hear. Then she took a deep breath, straightened her shoulders and marched toward them.

THREE

No record of Tabitha McConnell ever giving birth.

No adoption records.

No evidence that there is any connection between Jubilee and your sister.

The words spilled out of the mouth of the stunning brunette who sat across the table from Quinn. Flawless skin, beautiful tailored suit, Special Agent Veronica Spellings looked like a model and acted exactly like what she was—a federal investigator. She'd arrived an hour ago, and she'd been all business ever since. Questions. Jotted notes. Sympathetic looks mixed with a few raised eyebrows.

"Take a look at this," she said, sliding a paper across August's kitchen table, her dark eyes devoid of emotion. She had short nails and long fingers, the diamond ring that glinted on her left hand almost gaudy in comparison to the woman's conservative suit.

Quinn lifted the paper, eyeing the colored photo of a pretty blonde, a tall red-haired man and an infant. The woman held the baby as though she wasn't quite comfortable with it, her smile a little forced. She had dark circles under her eyes and the look of someone who was deeply unhappy. Beside her, the man stood grinning at the camera. His hand cupped the woman's shoulder, and the joy in his face was undeniable.

"That's Megan and Daniel Boone Anderson, and their daughter, Kendal. The picture was taken a month before Megan and Kendal disappeared. Megan died a few months later. Kendal has been missing ever since."

"I'm sorry," Quinn murmured. She wasn't sure what else to say.

"That was five years ago. The baby would be Jubilee's age now. Mr. Anderson has moved on, of course. He has a family. Children, but he's still desperate to find his daughter. He's never stopped looking for her." Agent Spellings eyed Quinn expectantly.

Quinn knew she was supposed to respond. Maybe with a gasp or a denial—*No way! The baby in the picture isn't Jubilee.*

She couldn't deny what she didn't know, though.

She wanted to believe Tabitha, but the evidence Agent Spellings had laid out was undeniable. Up until Tabitha had moved to Nevada a year and a half ago, she hadn't had a child. Friends at her old apartment had never seen her with a little girl. Her coworkers hadn't ever heard her speak about being a mother.

The FBI had moved fast, gathering information a lot more quickly than Quinn ever could have, and the information indicated that Tabitha had lied.

Quinn couldn't deny it. She couldn't brush it under the carpet and pretend it didn't exist. But, she wouldn't regret the decision she'd made, either. Jubilee deserved to be with someone who loved her, who had been desperately seeking her for years. If she was Daniel Boone Anderson's child, she deserved to be part of his family.

"I'm sorry for what happened, but I don't know anything about it." She fingered the photo before sliding it back across August's kitchen table. She and Agent Spellings had been left alone in the room, a half dozen police officers and two other agents vacating the kitchen and escorting August and Malone out with them. A CPS caseworker had arrived and taken Jubilee into another part of the house.

Hopefully, she hadn't taken the little girl away.

Jubilee might not be her niece, but Quinn felt responsible for her.

"You're sorry, but do you understand the ramifications of what you and your sister have done?"

"Of course, I understand, but I had no reason to doubt my sister's story."

"Except that you hadn't seen her in years," Agent Spellings pointed out.

"She's family." That was it. All Quinn was going to say. If she needed a lawyer, she'd get one. Right now, she just wanted to be done and go home.

"I understand. I have sisters, too. I know how deep the bond can run." Agent Spellings sighed. "You're not in any trouble with us, Quinn, but we would like to speak with your sister."

"If I knew where she was, I'd tell you."

"I hope so." The agent switched gears, pulled something out of a briefcase. "We found this in your car." Agent Spellings set a manila envelope on the table, Tabitha's handwriting scrawled across the front. It had been sealed when Quinn fled the SUV. Now the flap was open.

"Tabitha gave it to me."

"And you didn't open it?"

"She asked me not to."

Agent Spellings raised a dark eyebrow. Obviously, she doubted Quinn's answer.

"She asked me to give it to Jubilee's father,"

Quinn continued, her tone a little more defensive than she wanted it to be.

"I would have been curious enough to open it," Agent Spellings countered. "Most people would have done the same."

"I'm not most people. Jubilee's father's contact information was on the envelope. I didn't have any need to see what was inside of it, and I had no reason to doubt my sister's word."

Agent Spellings snorted, the first time she'd done anything that was less than professional. "Of course you did. Your sister is as much of a con artist as your father was."

It was a low blow, and one Quinn wasn't expecting. Obviously, Jubilee and Tabitha weren't the only ones the FBI had been investigating.

"What does that have to do with anything?" she hedged, not sure where the conversation was going but certain she wasn't going to like it.

"Did you really think she wasn't conning you, Quinn? That she didn't know you were going to become bait? A way of getting whoever was after her off her tail?"

"All I know is that she was dead serious when she said she was afraid of her husband. She wasn't conning me when she said he'd kill her when he found her."

"Believing people we love is a lot easier than realizing we've been fooled and used by them."

"I'm not a fool, Agent Spellings. Living with my father taught me how to know a lie from the truth."

Agent Spellings sighed. "Then, maybe she was afraid but maybe it was because she took thousands of dollars from her husband's bank account and stole a small fortune worth of family jewelry from his wall safe."

"Who told you she did that?"

"A police report was filed in Las Vegas last night. We're trying to get in touch with your sister's husband now. He flew out of town on business a few hours after he filed the report."

"Convenient," Quinn muttered, but she felt exactly like what Agent Spellings had implied she was—tricked, duped, used.

"The trip had been scheduled for months, Quinn. As a matter of fact, your sister's husband was supposed to leave yesterday morning. His flight was delayed, then canceled. He booked a second flight out late last night. I'm sure your sister wasn't anticipating him coming home so soon and discovering what she'd stolen."

"Has it occurred to you that she took what she did, because she was terrified, and she needed a way to start a new life?"

"Even if that was true—" and based on the way Agent Spellings looked when she said it, she didn't think it was "—there's no reasonable or acceptable excuse for committing a crime. I'm sure you know that, Quinn."

She did, but she didn't think Agent Spellings expected a response, so she kept her mouth shut.

"Like I said," Agent Spellings continued, "you're not in any kind of trouble. We know you were doing a favor for your sister, and we know that you had no idea the child you were transporting wasn't hers. If you'd opened the envelope your sister gave you, you might have realized that before you traveled six hundred miles." She pulled a sheet of paper from the envelope, slid it toward Quinn. "This is Kendal Grace Anderson's birth certificate. The original."

"Oh," was all she could manage, the official document sitting in front of her all the evidence she needed that Tabitha had had no business taking Jubilee anywhere.

"Your sister lied to you, Quinn. Jubilee was never her child. I'm sorry about that, but you can help us find out how Tabitha ended up with someone else's child, and you can help us figure out how this document got into her hands."

"And help send my sister to prison, right? That's what you're asking me to do," she said, the words tasting like dust on her tongue.

"*If* your sister kidnapped a child, then she's sent herself to prison."

"I know."

"Then don't feel guilty about helping us with the investigation. Mr. Anderson has every right to know whether or not Jubilee is his. If she is, he has every right to know how she ended up in your sister's custody."

"I've told you everything I know. I gave one of the responding police officers Tabitha's cell phone number. I told him where Tabitha said she was going."

"Florida, right?"

"Yes."

"She told you she booked a flight?"

"Yes."

"We've checked the airports. She didn't have a ticket."

Another lie. They were piling up, and there was nothing Quinn could do but accept it. "I wish I had more information. I've told you everything I know."

"If you think of anything else, let me know. If she contacts you, I need to know immediately. We're trying to trace her cell phone."

"Okay."

"Sit tight," Agent Spelling said. "I'll be back in a few minutes." She walked out of the room, and Quinn was left alone, the soft tick of a clock and the quiet murmur of voices background music to the wild thumping of her heart.

She had been lied to.

She'd believed the lie.

She could toss in the towel, admit that her sister was a kidnapper, a thief, a con artist, and maybe those things really were true. But Tabitha had been terrified. There'd been no doubt about that. She'd been bruised, too. A faded black eye, a healing cut on her lip.

Quinn should have called the police the minute Tabitha told her that her husband and caused the marks, but Tabitha had begged her not to. Too dangerous. Her husband was too well connected. He knew people in high places.

Had it all been a lie to cover Tabitha's crimes?

Given Tabitha's history, it was an easy thing to believe, but Quinn didn't believe it.

She'd seen terror in her sister's eyes.

She couldn't discount it. She wouldn't.

Family first. That's what her mother had taught Quinn. Always. Husband, kids. They'd all been a priority to Alison McConnell. Everyone first. Alison last. The stress of that had made Alison age well before she should have.

Quinn grabbed the cup of coffee her brother had poured an hour ago, surprised by the direction of her thoughts. Her mother had been gone for a decade. Her death had been the catalyst that had spurred Quinn to get her teaching degree. That had always been Alison's dream—

to teach children, but she'd put it on hold to marry and raise her children. Quinn had loved her mother for that. Her father? She'd tried.

She took a sip of cold coffee, wiped a splotch of condensation from the mug. She knew what her mother would want her to do, would expect her to do. Go back to Echo Lake, retrace her steps, try to figure out where Tabitha had gone. Alison would want Quinn to find out the truth about her sister, and then she'd want her to help her sister make things right.

Because Quinn had always been the sibling who followed the rules, did things the right way, tried to make everyone happy. She'd do it again this time. She owed her mother—for all the love she'd given her, for the money she'd set aside in a savings account for Quinn's college. She owed her for teaching her the value of faith and the importance of love, because if Quinn had only had her father as an example, she'd have learned that people were there to be used, that family was there as a cover for criminal activity.

Even if she hadn't owed her mother, she'd have gone looking for Tabitha. She needed to know the truth, and she needed to know her sister was safe.

She carried the coffee to the sink and poured

it out. She needed to get her Jeep, get her purse, head back home.

"Everything okay in here?" a man said, the voice so unexpected she jumped, whirling toward the doorway.

Malone stood on the threshold, his broad shoulders nearly filling the space, the scar on his face deep red-purple.

"You scared a year off my life."

"Sorry," he said easily.

"It wouldn't matter so much if I hadn't already had ten years scared off back in the woods."

"Sorry about that, too." He had the darkest eyes she'd ever seen. Not quite black, but close. And he didn't smile. Not even a hint of it.

"You probably saved my life, so I guess an apology isn't necessary."

He nodded, his gaze dropping from her face to the bright pink t-shirt she'd chosen for the trip. Dozens of little hand prints were splattered across it in various colors. A Christmas gift from last year's kindergarten class. On anyone else, it would have been fine, but it made Quinn look even younger than she already did.

"I'm a teacher," she said, tugging her sweatshirt closed, her cheeks hot.

"I know."

"The kids gave me this shirt last year."

"No explanation necessary."

"I wasn't explaining."

"Actually," he said, something that might have been humor gleaming in his eyes, "you were."

"Okay. I was. Agent Spellings just finished interrogating me. I'm a little frazzled."

"She'd probably prefer to refer to it as an interview."

"Whatever it was, I'm frazzled."

"You shouldn't be. You haven't done anything wrong. You've got nothing to hide. You've got no reason to be worried about speaking with law enforcement."

"That's what she said."

"Did she say anything else?" he asked, and she knew there was something specific he wanted to know. Maybe about Jubilee and her biological father.

"She said a lot of things. Most of them were about my sister and not very flattering."

"I'd apologize, but your sister has done a pretty good job of making herself look bad."

"I know."

"Did Agent Spellings ask when you realized you were being followed?"

"Yes."

"And?"

"Is this your version of an interrogation?"

"I prefer to refer to it as an interview," he said, and she almost laughed.

Almost.

Except there was nothing to laugh about.

Her sister was in trouble.

She was in trouble.

Jubilee's entire life was about to be turned upside down.

"As far as I know, they started following me right before I hit New York."

"You're sure they didn't follow you from home?"

"Agent Spellings asked me that, too, and I gave her the same answer I'll give you—I'm sure. I would have noticed if they'd started following me earlier. There's not much between Echo Lake and Boston."

"It seems odd that they were able to pick up your trail so far from home, don't you think?"

She hadn't thought. Not about that, and Agent Spellings hadn't mentioned it. She'd been too busy asking questions about Tabitha's life. Questions Quinn hadn't been able to answer.

"I guess it is."

"It makes me think that someone besides Tabitha knew her plans."

"No way. She was scared out of her mind. She wouldn't have told anyone anything."

"Not a friend? A lover?"

She hesitated, then shook her head. "No."

"You're not sure, Quinn. We both know it." He said it kindly, but she heard the accusation in his words the same way she'd heard them in Agent Spellings'.

"You're right. I'm not. My sister and I hadn't spoken in years. I sent her Christmas cards and birthday cards and hoped they'd be forwarded to whatever place she'd moved to. I never got anything in response. I didn't even know if she had my address. Then, she showed up on my doorstep, terrified. Was I supposed to turn her away?"

"No. You weren't," he said simply. "She was terrified of her husband, right?"

"Yes. She said he would be following her, trying to get her back. She also said he wouldn't care about Jubilee."

"I guess that wasn't the truth."

"There were a lot of things she said that weren't the truth." She didn't want to discuss them, though. Not until she could wrap her mind around what her sister had done. Taken a child that wasn't hers or her husbands? If that were the truth, how had Jubilee ended up in Las Vegas with them?

"Have you seen Jubilee?" She changed the subject, because that was easier than discussing her sister's mistakes.

"She's back in one of the bedrooms with a couple of CPS workers. I tried to get in, but it was a no-go. They've got her guarded tighter than Fort Knox."

"When will her father be here?"

"Boone? Not for another twenty-something hours. If he's her father. We haven't established that yet. I'm hoping you can help me out, though."

"How?"

"I heard a couple of the CPS workers talking about a birth certificate. Have you seen it?" There was no emotion in his voice, none on his face, but she could feel the energy in him, could sense his tension.

This was what he'd come into the kitchen to find out, and she had no reason to keep the truth from him. "Yes. It was in the envelope my sister gave me."

He stilled, his dark eyes spearing into hers. "You got a good look at it?"

"I saw her father's name and her mother's."

"And?"

"Your friend was listed as her biological father. Which matches with what my sister told me." The one truth among the many lies.

"You don't seem happy about it."

"I'm not happy about any of this. The FBI seems to think Tabitha has been keeping a missing child for years. She may end up in jail and poor Jubilee—"

"Will be back with her father. Where she belongs."

"It is a rough thing for a child to be pulled away from everything she knows."

"It is just as rough a thing for a man to be without his child for five years," he responded.

"*If* she's his child." But, she really didn't doubt that Jubilee was.

"I saw her when we walked in the house. She looks just like him. A prettier, younger, cuter version, but just like him." He grabbed a mug from a small stack near the coffeemaker. Small scars crisscrossed his knuckles, thin white lines against his tan skin. They were nothing like the scar on his face. That one was thick and jagged, stretching from the corner of his eye to his jaw.

"And there's the birth certificate," she said more to herself than to him. How had Tabitha gotten her hands on it? If Jubilee wasn't Daniel Boone Anderson's child, why had Tabitha asked her to bring the little girl to him?

"There's that, too. Wonder where your sister got it." His voice had gone quiet, his eyes suddenly cold and hard.

"I don't know."

"I may just have to see if I can find her. Boone deserves the truth."

"So does everyone else, but you're just going to have to join the crowd of people hoping to get it, because I have nothing else to offer."

"Except that you're the one person your sister has contacted since she left Las Vegas."

"There's that," she murmured, grabbing a clean coffee cup and filling it with hot liquid. She took a sip. It tasted like sawdust and disappointment.

This was what Malone had been hoping to hear. A birth certificate with Boone's name on it. It was the kind of thing that he'd been looking for. Not just a red-haired child with freckles and blue eyes. A document that linked that child with Boone.

He needed to track down Special Agent Spellings and confirm that the birth certificate was legit, then he'd call Chance. His boss had left DC nearly three hours ago. He'd be arriving soon, but this wasn't the kind of news that Malone wanted to hold on to. The sooner they could confirm the birth certificate, the sooner they could start the process of petitioning CPS to run DNA tests. Five years was a long time to wait to be reunited with a loved one. He didn't want Boone to have to wait even an hour longer.

Once he got the information about the birth certificate, he was going to do a little digging, see if he could figure out where Tabitha had gone. He wanted to talk to her.

So did a host of other people. Quinn was right about that. She was wrong about her sister, though. Tabitha had known exactly what she was getting Quinn into.

He was pretty certain that Quinn realized it now.

Too little, too late.

She was staring into her coffee cup as if she could find the mysteries of the universe in it, the bright pink hand-printed shirt peeking out from beneath her sweatshirt again.

She didn't look angry. She looked…sad.

That bothered Malone more than he wanted it to.

A simple mission. In. Out. Back to his vacation. Only it wasn't going to turn out that way. He set his mug down, took Quinn's.

"You were right," he said, placing it next to his.

"About what?"

"Everything is going to be okay."

"I didn't say that."

"Sure you did. You said it to Jubilee."

She frowned, her smooth skin and large gray eyes making her look years younger than she was. She could have passed for a teenager, but he knew she'd been widowed for several years. He'd have liked to know more.

Like why a woman as smart as she seemed to be would believe the lies her sister had told her.

"I guess I did." She offered a half smile and sighed. "I probably knew Tabitha wasn't telling me the entire truth, but I never would have imagined that she had a child who wasn't hers."

"We could all be mistaken. That's a possibility."

"No. It's not. I got a good look at the birth certificate. It was an original," she responded.

"Did you see the baby's name?"

"Kendal Grace Anderson." Flyaway strands of hair stuck to her forehead and cheek. She brushed them away, moved toward the back door. "Mother's name was Megan. Father's name Daniel Boone Anderson."

It all lined up.

Every detail.

"I need to call my boss," he muttered. Once Boone got word about the birth certificate, he was going to be chomping at the bit, trying to get home faster than humanly possible. Returning home and being told he wasn't going to be able to see his child wouldn't sit well. Maybe Chance could work a little magic and make sure that didn't happen.

"You go ahead. I…need some air." Quinn

walked to a small alcove at the back of the kitchen. A door led from there out to a porch.

Malone had already scouted the property, looking for areas that might be security risks. Quinn had been run off the road and chased into the woods. There was no guarantee the perpetrator wouldn't return, but there were law enforcement officers all over the property and along the road where Quinn's Jeep had been abandoned. She'd be fine outside on her own, but he followed anyway, stepping into the cool night air.

"You don't have to babysit me," Quinn murmured as she settled onto a bench swing that hung from porch eaves.

"Who said I was?" He settled down beside her, the chains creaking.

"You were going to call your boss."

"It can wait."

"Until?"

"I make sure you're okay."

"Why wouldn't I be?" She pulled her knees up to her chest and wrapped her arms around her legs. She was tiny. Probably a foot shorter than Malone, but her personality seemed bigger—her voice, her gestures, those eyes that seemed to take up most of her face.

"You were lied to. You were put in danger. You trusted someone, and you were betrayed."

They were all good reasons for not being okay, but Quinn shrugged.

"I've been through worse."

"I'm sorry for that."

She turned her head, looked him straight in the eyes, her gaze dropping to the scar on his cheek, the one on his hands. "I think you've been through way worse, so I don't think you should be sorry for me."

"Trouble is relative." He stood and paced to the porch railing, because he didn't want her to ask about the scars. It wasn't something he discussed—the torture, the sorrow of losing brothers in arms, the helplessness of watching it happen. "Is there someone you want me to call?"

"About?"

"You. Your brother is busy with the police. I thought you might want some moral support."

"If my husband were alive," she said quietly, "I'd want him here. He's not, and there's no one else."

"I'll say I'm sorry again. For your loss, this time."

"Thanks."

"I know it doesn't change anything."

"It doesn't, but after a while, the agony fades to a dull ache."

He'd been there. Done that. He knew how

it felt to lose someone and to move on from it. The ache never left. It simply became tolerable.

"Quinn—" he began, not really sure what he was going to say, not actually sure he should say anything.

They were strangers, and nothing he could say to her would make any difference.

"Are you going to let Daniel know about the birth certificate?" She cut him off.

"Daniel?" he asked, confused for a split second before the name registered. "Boone. That's what he goes by. I'll send him a text. Our boss will, too."

"Boss?"

"Chance Miller. He owns HEART."

"I'd like to say I've heard of it."

"But you haven't? Neither have most people. We're a privately owned hostage rescue team. We also provide security, do cyber forensics. Lots of things."

"Including tracking down a coworker's missing child?"

"That, too." He stood, the swing creaking as it moved. "Hopefully, this will all pan out. I'd hate for Boone to get his hopes up and then have them dashed."

"I have a feeling it will. I just hope that it pans out for Jubilee, too. She deserves to have a happy ending, because I don't think her beginning has been easy."

"I saw the bruise on her cheek."

"There are a few on her arms, too. And, she doesn't talk. Boone will have his work cut out for him."

"He's up for it. He's been waiting for this for five years, preparing for it."

"Maybe you can give me a call after they meet, let me know how it goes."

"You could stick around. Find out for yourself."

"I need to get back to Echo Lake. I've got a job, a whole classroom full of kindergartners who won't know what to do if I'm not there."

"You like the little kids, huh?"

"I do, but it's also the only grade that I could be guaranteed to be taller than all my pupils."

That surprised a laugh out of him, and she smiled. "Yeah, it was a joke, but I have met third graders who are almost as tall as me."

The back door opened, and August stepped outside.

"I've been looking for you, Quinn. Is everything okay out here?" he asked.

"Just waiting to get permission to go home," she responded.

"You have it. The authorities have your contact information, and Agent Spellings said you're free to go when you're ready."

"I'm ready." She stood. "I've just got to get my Jeep…"

"I drove it here," August said. "But I think you should stay until the sun comes up."

"It's almost up now," she responded. "And the sooner I get on the road, the sooner I can get home. I've got a classroom full of rowdy five-year-olds to face on Monday morning."

"A few hours isn't going to make a difference," August responded. "I have a few things to tie up here before I can go, and I'd prefer you to wait until we can leave together."

She frowned. "Why would we leave together?"

"Because, I want to make sure you stay safe."

"Safe from what? The guys who ran me off the road wanted to get Jubilee. She's in protective custody until her father returns. They've got no further use for me."

"No?" Malone interrupted, because he agreed with August. Quinn shouldn't be going anywhere alone. Not until they knew exactly what was going on. "Has it occurred to you that they wanted Jubilee because they thought having her would help them get to your sister?"

"I can't think of any other reason why they would want her, so yes. It's occurred to me."

"Now that she's in protective custody, they'll want another pawn that they can use. That makes you a likely target," he pointed out, and she scowled.

"They don't even know who I am, and there's no way they're hanging around anywhere close by to watch for my Jeep. They're long gone, and if I leave now, I will be, too. If they come back after the police and FBI are gone, they'll be too late to follow me. I'll be home safe and sound in Echo Lake and all of this will be over."

Malone hoped she was right, but he didn't think she could count on it. Desperate people did desperate things. That included kidnapping people they thought could be beneficial to their cause.

"If you're right, I'll apologize later. For now, how about we just agree that you'll stay until I can leave with you?" August suggested.

"I don't need—"

"*I* do," August cut her off. "You're my kid sister. I couldn't live with myself if I let something happen to you."

"Fine. I won't leave until you can," she said.

"Glad to know I can still win my battles with you. I put your purse in the guest room. Here's your phone. Looks like you've got a couple of messages. You recognize the number?"

She took it, looked at the screen. "I think this

is the one Tabitha gave me. I was in a hurry and didn't add it to my contacts list."

"Hopefully, the messages explain the mess she's gotten you into," August muttered.

"You're assuming she knows that she got me into a mess."

"Trust me, kid. She knows."

"I'm not a kid," Quinn said absently as she pressed a button and held the phone to her ear. "Nothing on the first one. Let's see if she left a message the second time." Her eyes widened, and she motioned for August to move closer.

Malone didn't wait for an invitation. He bent down, his head so close to Quinn's that her hair brushed his cheek. He could hear what sounded like a masculine voice, the words chilling.

"You want to see your sister again? You bring that kid back home." Seconds later, a woman screamed, the sound filled with so much terror, Malone wanted to jump through the phone to save her.

August must have felt the same.

He snatched the phone from Quinn's hand and listened to the message again, wincing when the woman screamed.

"If that's Tabitha…"

"I know it's her phone number," Quinn said, staring at the phone as if it were going to jump out of his hand and attack her. "They must have found her."

"We need to hand this over to the FBI," Malone said, taking the phone from August's hand.

"What if—?" Quinn began.

"Let's save the questions for later." Malone grabbed her hand and pulled her toward the door. He didn't want to waste time. The call had come in half an hour ago. If the FBI could get a ping off the cell phone, they might be able to track the caller. "The longer we wait, the more chance the perpetrator has to leave the area he made the call from."

"The longer we wait, the more unlikely it's going to be that we'll find *Tabitha*," Quinn corrected.

If Tabitha was with the caller.

It was her phone, but that didn't mean she was near it.

It didn't mean she'd been the one screaming.

It didn't mean she was even alive.

Malone wasn't going to share any of those thoughts with Quinn.

"Right," he said instead as he pulled her into the house.

FOUR

The scream seemed to echo through Quinn's head as Malone hurried her into the living room. Several people stood there. Special Agent Spellings, two uniformed officers and a man dressed in jeans and a flannel shirt who, Quinn was pretty sure, was from CPS.

He smiled, gave a slight nod of acknowledgment. No one else seemed pleased that she, Malone and August had barged into the meeting.

"I guess you didn't hear that you have permission to return home," Agent Spellings said impatiently, her gaze on Malone. "You *all* have permission to go wherever you need to be. We have things secure here."

"I guess you didn't hear that this is my home, and the sheriff asked me to stick around until they finish searching the woods. I'm not planning to wait outside to make you people happy," August responded, a hint of anger in his voice.

"My apologies for taking over the way we have, but this is a missing child's case—a *kidnapped* child. Things need to be handled a certain way."

"There's been a threat made against Quinn's sister. I think that's important enough to interrupt your meeting," Malone said.

"What kind of threat?" Agent Spellings frowned, every hair still in place, her suit still wrinkle-free. Even after the hours she'd spent traveling and conducting interviews, she looked perfect.

She didn't look convinced, though.

She hadn't been convinced earlier, either.

She believed Tabitha was guilty of a crime or crimes, and Quinn didn't believe that a recorded scream was going to change her mind.

"I can play it for you," Quinn offered.

Agent Spellings nodded, and Quinn played the message—the male voice, the threat, the scream.

She shivered, but Agent Spellings looked unconcerned.

"The scream sounds exactly like a sound effect app one of my nephews likes to use to scare me."

"Are you saying she staged a kidnapping?" Quinn demanded.

"I'm saying that I'd like to have the message

analyzed. Do you mind if I take your phone?"
She held out her hand, and Quinn handed it
over.

"Tabitha would never fake something like
this."

"And she wouldn't take a child that didn't be-
long to her? Bring that child to her sister? Convince her sister to help her transport the child
across state lines?"

Ouch. That hurt, but Quinn wasn't going to
give up. Tabitha needed help. She was certain
of it.

"How long will it take you to decide if the
scream is real?" she asked.

"I'm certain that it's a real scream. We're
going to be trying to determine whether it was
dubbed in. A recording of a recording, so to
speak." She smiled.

Obviously, she wasn't taking the threat seriously.

No way was Quinn going to wait around
while the message was *analyzed*. She was getting her stuff, getting in her Jeep and heading
back to Echo Lake. With or without her brother.
There had to be a way to trace her sister's path
from there. Tabitha had arrived in a rental car. A
sporty black car that she'd parked right in front
of the building that housed Quinn's apartment.
She'd handed Quinn a booster seat, a pink back-

pack and the envelope before she'd left. It had been too dark for Quinn to read the license plate number, but whatever rental company Tabitha used would want the vehicle back eventually. If Quinn could find the company, she might be able to find her sister.

"You okay?" Malone asked, touching her elbow.

"I will be once I know my sister is okay."

"You can trust us to do that," Agent Spellings assured her.

But trust was a difficult thing for Quinn; trusting strangers was nearly impossible. She'd learned to take care of herself years ago. That had served her well when Cory became ill. She'd been able to care for him and for herself. She'd known how to make do, how to solve problems. How to fix things.

Except for Cory's health.

That she hadn't been able to fix no matter how hard she'd tried.

"Right. Trust," she murmured. "I'll do that. Is there any way I can see Jubilee? I'd like to say goodbye before I leave."

"We agreed that we're leaving together," August reminded her.

She ignored him.

Waiting wasn't going to help Tabitha.

"I'm sorry," the guy she'd pegged for CPS

said. "She's been through a lot, and we think it would be better if—"

"It would probably be better for that poor girl to have a chance to say goodbye," Agent Spellings cut in, offering support that Quinn hadn't expected. "She's had too many adults disappear from her life. I think we can all agree that's not healthy for a child."

"Well—" the guy frowned "—it isn't, but nothing that has happened to her is healthy."

"I'm not going to traumatize her more," Quinn assured him. "I just want to say goodbye."

"I guess it won't hurt. Come on." He led her down the hall and into one of August's guest rooms. It was small, just enough space in it to house a dresser, a twin bed and a night stand.

Two women stood near a window. One held a clipboard. The other had a phone. Both looked tired and a little frazzled.

"John," the taller of the two said. "Didn't we agree that Jubilee shouldn't be disturbed?"

"This is her aunt," he explained.

"Not legally," the woman responded. "I'm sorry, Ms....?"

"Robertson."

"Ms. Robertson, I'm Anna Smith, Jubilee's caseworker. She is terrified. She's decided that the closet is the safest place, and we want her to feel safe, don't we?" She sounded as if she were speaking to a child. It rubbed Quinn the wrong way, but she'd play nice if it meant seeing Jubilee.

"Of course. I plan to return to Maine, though, and I thought—"

A soft thump interrupted her words.

Seconds later, the closet door creaked open, and Jubilee peeked out, her eyes red, her cheeks wet.

She'd been crying.

Poor kid.

"Hey, kiddo." Quinn crouched and held out her arms. "Got a hug for me?"

"She doesn't like to be touched," Anna informed her, but Jubilee had already moved forward and was throwing herself into Quinn's arms.

"It's okay," Quinn murmured, smoothing silky curls from hot sticky cheeks. "You're going to be okay."

Tears rolled down Jubilee's cheeks, silent sobs wracking her body.

"What's wrong, kiddo? Are you scared or sad?"

"She doesn't speak." Anna had moved in, hovering nearby as if she were afraid Quinn was going to grab the child and run.

"Can you find Mommy?" Jubilee asked, the

words clear and crisp. They were the first words she'd spoken, and Quinn couldn't quite grasp that they'd actually come out of her mouth.

"What?" she asked, and Jubilee pressed her palms to Quinn's face, looked straight into her eyes.

"I need you to find Mommy."

"I will," she said, shocked at how mature Jubilee sounded, how articulate she was. She'd assumed there was a learning disability or some emotional reason the little girl didn't speak. Apparently, she simply hadn't wanted to.

"Promise?"

"Of course." The words slipped out before she could think them through, the promise made so quickly, she almost didn't realize she'd made it. "I'm going back to the place we last saw her. When I find her, I'll make sure she knows how much you want to see her."

"It will be up to Jubilee's birth father to decide if seeing each other is a good idea," Anna cautioned, and tears began running down Jubilee's face again.

Quinn wiped them away, her hands shaking with fatigue, worry, frustration. "Honey, don't cry. Your dad is going to want what's best for you, and seeing your mother—"

"Not legally her mother," Anna reiterated.

"I don't think that matters to her."

Anna ignored the comment, crouching down and touching the little girl's arm. "We've talked about this."

Jubilee jerked away, pressing closer to Quinn.

Anna sighed. "You know that we're looking for your real father. I explained this. He has been waiting a very long time to see you again, and he—"

Jubilee walked back into the closet and shut the door.

"She's very upset," Anna explained as if it weren't obvious. "This is too much for a five-year-old to handle."

"It would be too much for most people to handle." Quinn answered by rote, her mind on the promise she'd made.

The one she couldn't break.

Wouldn't break.

She'd said she'd find Tabitha. It's what she wanted anyway. Now she not only had to find her sister, she had to make sure that Jubilee's birth father was willing to let the two be reunited.

One bridge at a time.

That's all she had to cross.

First, she'd find Tabitha and make certain she was safe. Then, she'd figure out how to reunite the two.

"I'd better go," she said. "Maine is a long drive. I'll leave you with my contact information—"

"We have it," Anna said with a forced smile. "Do you have a card, so I can reach you?"

The woman dug into her purse, took out a card and handed it to her. "That's my direct number. I know my methods may seem abrupt, but I've worked with traumatized kids for years. Most of the time, it's best to get them back into structure and security quickly."

"I understand. Thanks for letting me see her. I'll be in touch."

She walked out of the room, her heart beating hollowly in her chest.

What had Tabitha gotten herself into?

And how in the world was Quinn going to get her out of it?

Nothing is impossible with God.

How many times had her mother said that?

During the difficult times, the struggles, the financial crises, her faith had never wavered. Until the end, she'd never stopped believing that God was going to come through.

Quinn didn't think she had her mother's faith.

Hers was tired, fragile, weak. It felt used up and old and tethered to her by years of spouting prayers and Christian platitudes. Did she really believe that nothing was impossible when God was in it?

She wanted to.

She really did, because she was going to Maine. Now. With or without her brother's approval.

Quinn was going to leave, and she wasn't going to wait a few hours to do it. Malone had seen the look on her face, the fear in her eyes, and then the frustration when Agent Spellings hadn't seemed to take the phone call and threat seriously. She *was* taking it seriously. The FBI didn't mess around. They'd play it safe, make sure that they were on the right track, and then they'd act.

Malone could have told Quinn that, but she wouldn't have believed him. It was *her* sister who was missing. If he were standing in Quinn's shoes, he'd leave, too.

The question was, would she leave through the front door or try to sneak out without her brother noticing?

He glanced at August. The guy was deep in a discussion with law enforcement. Apparently, Tabitha had rented a car in Maine and returned it four hours after she'd left Jubilee with Quinn. Law enforcement was trying to figure out where she'd gone during those four hours, who'd she'd seen, who she might have contacted. Where she'd gone after.

Did she get a ride with someone?

Take the bus?

Stay near Echo Lake?

All good questions, and they needed answers, but there was no way Quinn was going to wait around while they figured it out. There was no way Malone was letting her drive up to Maine by herself. He'd come because of Jubilee, but he never quit until a mission was complete. In his mind, this wouldn't be complete until he knew everyone involved was safe.

He didn't like the feel of things.

He didn't like the phone call, the scream, the fact that Tabitha's phone might be in someone else's hands. He especially didn't like the idea that Quinn might be walking into a trap, that she might be used as a pawn to get to Jubilee or Tabitha.

Whichever one the perpetrator was really going after.

That was the question Malone was most interested in answering. Who was the real target?

He texted Chance the information he had— birth certificate, kid with red hair and blue eyes. Tabitha's husband's name. His city of residence. Chance was always quick with solutions. He'd start digging into Jarrod Williams's life, find out if there was any reason to doubt the story he'd told the police.

People lied. All the time.

It would be interesting to see if Jarrod had.

Malone shoved the phone into his pocket and walked out of the room. No one seemed to notice. Just like no one would probably notice if Quinn slipped out under the radar.

In her position, it's probably what he'd do.

He walked down a wide hall, glanced into an open doorway—a white bathroom with tiled floor and walls. There were three other rooms, all of them with their doors closed.

He knocked on the first one, and a wide-eyed brunette opened it just enough for him to get a glimpse of the tiny room beyond.

"I'm sorry. No one can see Jubilee," she said sharply.

"I'm looking for Quinn."

"She left a couple of minutes ago."

"Left?"

"The room," she said with a tired sigh. "I don't know where she went after that."

She closed the door before he could respond.

He thought about knocking again, trying to get a glimpse of Jubilee, but Quinn had gone somewhere. Not into the kitchen. She'd have had to walk through the living room to do that.

He knocked on the second door, waited a moment and opened it. Dark furniture—bed, desk, curtains. It looked like August's room. He went to the third. Knocked.

"Quinn?" he called.

She didn't respond, so he tried the knob. It turned easily, a draft of cold air sweeping out as he opened the door.

Curtains billowed at a wide window, the air tinged with the hint of fall. He could smell pine needles, wood burning stove, something flowery and light that might have been the remnants of perfume.

He scanned the room. An open door led into a tiny closet. No place Quinn could have gone except out through the window.

He climbed out, stepping into thick hedges that had already been smashed, their branches broken.

"Quinn," he called, his voice sharp.

She'd be heading around the house by now, looking for the Jeep. The one that her brother still had the keys to. Malone had seen a #1 Teacher key chain dangling out of August's back pocket while he was talking to the police.

He jogged to the front of the house. The Jeep was at the end of the driveway, someone standing beside the driver's door.

"Your brother has the key," he called as he walked toward it.

"I wish I'd known that before I'd decided to

climb out the window," Quinn muttered, her face pale in the darkness.

"You wouldn't have had to climb out a window if you'd walked out the front door, and if you'd done that, your brother would have told you he had the key."

"He'd also have insisted on coming with me."

"What's wrong with that?"

"I don't want to wait around for him to finish whatever it is he has to do."

"You'd rather put yourself in danger?"

"Tabitha is in danger. That is paramount to everything right now."

"You can't save your sister by getting yourself kidnapped or killed, Quinn. You're running on emotion. You need to slow down and start thinking."

"I am thinking, and what I'm thinking is that sitting here twiddling my thumbs isn't doing Tabitha any good. I couldn't live with myself if something happened to her because I waited until the sun came up."

"You won't be able to live with yourself if you're dead, either."

She smiled at that, a quick curve of her lips that was there and gone so quickly he almost didn't see it. "You've got a point, but I still want to leave."

"Then, let's go, but let's do it the right way."

"Which is?"

"We tell your brother. We tell my boss, and then I ride up to Maine with you."

"I think you have better things to do with your time." But, she hiked her purse onto her shoulder and started walking back to the house.

"Like?"

"Work? Family? Life?"

"I'm on vacation, and my family consists of a bunch of siblings and cousins who are all perfectly capable of taking care of themselves."

"*This* is what you do on vacation?"

"This is what I do for my job. I got asked to help because I was vacationing in a cabin close by."

"You could go back to the cabin, then, and finish what you started."

"I'm going to finish what I started here first."

"You came because of Jubilee," she reminded him, stepping onto the porch, light spilling onto her hair and face.

"And, I'm staying because of you. Until I know everyone involved is safe, this assignment isn't complete."

"Everyone you've had any contact with *is* safe."

"For now," he muttered, scanning the darkness beyond the yard, because something was crawling along his spine—a whisper of danger, a warning that trouble might be closing in again.

"I don't—"

"Let's discuss it inside."

"Why—?"

There was a flash of light in the trees to their right. Malone was moving before it registered, tackling Quinn, bringing her down hard. Too hard.

Something slammed into the porch railing, splintering wood and sending shrapnel flying. Another flash, and a window shattered, some- one inside shouting a warning.

The porch light went off, and they were plunged into darkness. August. Or one of the law enforcement officers, providing cover. Malone was going to take advantage of it. He rolled toward the edge of the porch, dragging Quinn with him, the sound of a car engine breaking through the deadly quiet.

Chance finally arriving?

He hoped so.

They needed backup, and they needed it soon.

The front door flew open, and August stepped out, his arm raised, a gun pointed toward the darkness.

"To the right," Malone shouted, and August fired one round after another into the darkness.

FIVE

Seconds. That's how long it took from the first shot to the last. It felt like an eternity to Quinn. The ground seemed to shake as law enforcement officers stormed out of the house and headed into the woods.

Was August okay?

Jubilee?

She tried to raise her head, but Malone's heavy weight held her in place, his entire body pressing her into the ground.

"Stay still," he growled.

"August—"

"Is fine."

"What about Jubilee?"

"I don't know."

"I need to find out."

"You need to stay down."

She would have argued, but she could barely catch enough breath to do it. His weight or panic, she didn't know which, but she was gasping for air, black spots dancing at the edge of her vision.

Suddenly, Malone shifted, rolling onto his side, positioning himself between Quinn and the yard. They were face-to-face now, the scar black in the darkness, his eyes gleaming. "You okay?"

"Now that I can breathe, I am," she responded, pushing onto her elbows, then her knees. She needed to stand, but she felt wobbly, every muscle trembling.

"Sorry about that." He got to his feet, lithe and oddly graceful, and held out a hand to help her up.

Just like that, she was upright, still shaky, still trembling.

Still alive.

Thanks to Malone.

"I think you just saved my life," she said, and she could hear the shock in her voice, the terror. "Thank you."

"You might want to save your thanks until all this is over," he said as he hurried her into the house.

It wasn't over? she wanted to ask, but Malone closed the door and left her standing in the darkness.

Every light in the house had been turned off. Not a sound drifted into the living room.

Was she alone?

Should she turn on the lights?

Was it safe to do that?

Glass cracked under her feet as she moved through the room, bits of it glinting in the darkness.

"Hello?" she called, picking her way into the hallway. "Jubilee?"

"They just left with her," someone said, his voice calm and quiet. She jumped anyway, whirling toward the speaker. He was in the threshold of the guestroom. Tall. Lean. Muscular. She couldn't make out his face, but he didn't look like any of the officers, and that made her nervous.

"Where did you come from?"

"I crawled through an open window."

"Usually only criminals do that."

"Or people who are trying to get in a locked door. I helped escort the CPS team to a vehicle that was waiting out back. When I tried to get back in, the door was locked. I'm Chance Miller, by the way. From HEART."

"Malone's boss?"

"I prefer to call myself his coworker. Unless he's not listening to my instructions. Then I'm his boss."

"Does he usually listen?"

"What do you think?"

"No?"

"Exactly. Take tonight for example. I told Malone to check on Kendal Anderson and go back to his vacation. Instead, he's decided he needs to stick around."

"Jubilee," she corrected, because the five-year-old needed some consistency in her life, some constancy. She'd lost her birth mother. She'd lost her stepmother. She'd lost the guy who'd been raising her with Tabitha. She did not need to lose her name.

"Pardon?"

"She goes by Jubilee now."

"Right. I got the memo. I've been hearing the other name for so long, it rolls out without much thought. Sorry about that."

"You don't have to apologize to me, but someone sure does need to apologize to that little girl."

"You don't think that's your sister's responsibility?" No edge in his voice, but she thought she heard a note of censure.

"I don't think my sister kidnapped your friend's daughter, if that's what you're asking."

"I guess I might have been. Eventually Boone is going to need answers. Eventually Jubilee is going to be old enough and mature enough to need them, too."

"They both deserve to know the truth. I'm just not sure my sister is the one who has it."

"Sometimes a wait and see approach is best. How about we do that this time? Withhold judgment until we know the truth? You won't assume she doesn't know. I won't assume she does."

"Sounds good."

"You're an agreeable person, Quinn. I usually am, too. Which means we'll get along well for the next twelve hours."

"Twelve hours?"

"The drive up to Maine. That's about how long it takes."

"You're going to—?"

His phone buzzed, and he glanced at it. "Looks like we're ready to head out."

"To Maine?"

"Malone said you wanted to find your sister. My company is going to help you do that."

"Because you want to talk to her?"

"Because she might be in trouble, and getting people out of trouble is what HEART specializes in." The sincerity in his voice was undeniable, and she didn't resist as he urged her through the living room and out the front door.

Someone had parked an SUV near the porch, and Chance hurried her down the stairs and into the backseat.

She thought she'd be sitting near the door, but

he nudged her farther in, taking the seat next to the window.

She could have scooted over, but Malone was there, gazing out the side window, his attention so focused, she wasn't even sure he knew she was there.

She felt hemmed in and uncomfortable, sandwiched between two men who'd been strangers a few minutes ago. "I'm going to need my Jeep when I get to Echo Lake," she said, hoping they'd switch vehicles. She could drive the Jeep. The men would sit where they wanted.

"I've got another team member driving it up for you," Chance replied.

"You didn't think you should ask my permission first?"

"No." There was nothing agreeable about that one word, nothing that made her feel as if they were going to get along. As a matter of fact, Chance suddenly looked as hard and unapproachable as Malone.

"Is there some reason why we're not all going together?"

"The perpetrator knows what your vehicle looks like. We'd rather you not be in it, if he tries something while we're traveling."

"You don't want to risk my life, but you're willing to risk someone else's."

"It's a calculated risk," Malone murmured.

"She knows what she's doing, and she knows how to get out of trouble if she finds herself in it."

"She?"

"Stella Silverstone." Chance provided the name, a hint of something that sounded like irritation in his voice. "You should have checked with me before you sent her off in a bait car."

"I planned to. She took off while I was texting you," Malone said, and he didn't sound happy about it.

"She and I are going to have a serious talk when this is over."

"I think I've heard that one before," Malone grumbled. "How about you do this instead? Work on whatever problems the two of you have so you don't keep butting heads when we're on mission."

"We don't butt heads."

"Right, because you avoid each other. It's getting old."

"Not as old as this conversation."

Malone chuckled, the sound more annoyed than amused. "I figured you'd say that."

"And I figured that Stella would go running off again. I guess we were both right. Where's our driver? I don't want her getting too far ahead of us. Not with the trouble we've seen tonight."

"He had to answer a few questions."

"About?"

Malone's attention finally shifted, his gaze flitting to Quinn for a moment. "We can discuss it later."

That seemed to be code for something, because the conversation ended, time ticking away in silence. No tension in it. No resentment. The men seemed to know each other well enough to not be bothered by the other's comments.

Quinn, on the other hand, was bothered—by the silence, the stillness, the warmth of Malone's thigh pressed close to hers. By the fact that she noticed it.

The driver's-side door opened, and August climbed in. He had a smear of dirt on his cheek, a twig in his short hair. Blood on his shirt? It looked like it—the dark stain on his shoulder as black as ink.

"You're hurt!" She tried to lean over the seat to get a better look, but Malone pulled her back.

"Stay put."

"I need to see how bad it is."

"I've had worse," August spat. "And I've already bandaged it. Now, how about you do what Malone says and sit back?"

He shoved the keys into the ignition and rolled forward, the headlights off, the interior lights dimmed. He must think they were going to be ambushed. They must all think it. Why else would they be so tense? Why else would they insist she sit in the middle? Why else would they tell her not to lean forward?

If a bullet were aimed at the car, it would go through one of them before it hit her. That was their plan, and knowing it didn't make Quinn any happier about her situation. "I don't like this." She spoke into the silence, and August glanced into the rearview mirror, meeting her eyes for a nanosecond before he scanned the road again.

"What?"

"That the three of you are trying to stay between me and a gunman."

"We're trying to stay between you and death," August clarified, as if it weren't already clear enough.

"Stop the car. I'm getting out. Letting someone drive my car is one thing. Letting me cower in the center seat while you all put your lives at risk is another."

"I don't think that you understand how dangerous this is." Malone finally turned completely away from the window, his gaze so sharp, so intense that Quinn had to force herself to keep meeting his eyes.

"I understand exactly how dangerous it is. That's why I'm not going to let any of you do this."

"Yes. You are," Chance insisted.

"I thought you said you were agreeable?"

"Most of the time. This isn't one of them. There are three men trained in security in this car, and one woman who teaches kindergarten and, according to her brother, has never even taken a self-defense class. It stands to reason that the three will provide the firearm power and the one will use her brain to figure out how much sense that makes."

"I don't agree."

No response.

Not from any of the three men.

She opened her mouth to repeat herself, and Malone leaned in, his lips brushing her ear, the warmth of his breath fanning her cheek. For a moment, she was back in time, sitting in Cory's car during their first date, that little tickle of excitement in her belly because they were together. Only this guy wasn't Cory, and the excitement had no business being there.

Not now. Not ever, because she didn't want to go through heartache again. Not the kind she'd had while Cory was suffering. Not the kind that came after.

A guy like Malone might make her forget that, and then where would she be?

"I was kidding," he said quietly, his fingers gliding across her knuckles, that little shimmy of excitement filling her stomach again.

"I know," she responded, her throat tight with the memories of everything she'd lost, of all the things she missed.

"Then, maybe you also need to know that everything really is going to be okay." He repeated what he'd said before, what she'd said to Jubilee.

Maybe it was. Hopefully it was.

But, right then, it really didn't feel like it.

Quinn fell asleep just as the sun crested the trees. No more tension in her shoulders. No more taut, tight muscles in her thigh. One minute, she was ramrod straight. The next, she was slumped over, her head resting against Malone's shoulder.

"She's out," Chance commented idly as he scanned a text message. "And Stella is sixteen miles ahead of us. Clear roads. No traffic, and no sign that she's being followed."

"Too bad," August muttered. "If she had a tail, we could drop Quinn off and go have a little talk with whoever it is."

"I was thinking the same," Malone admitted. "Right now, we've got nothing to go on but speculation."

"We've got a dead gunman." August rolled his shoulders, grimacing as he moved. "And, I've got a six-inch gouge in my shoulder."

"You need medical attention?"

"No."

"Says the man who is still bleeding." Chance typed something into his phone. "Stella is looking for a place to pull over. Since she's a nurse, she can take care of the shoulder and I'll take care of the Jeep."

Malone wasn't surprised by the suggestion.

Chance and Stella might be at odds, but HEART was a family, the thread that connected the members unbreakable.

"I'm not bleeding." August touched his blood-stained sleeve. "Much."

Chance ignored the comment, his attention focused on his phone. "She said she's pulling off. Look for a boarded up farmhouse. North side of the road. Collapsing barn. It's the only building for a few dozen miles."

It didn't take long to cover the distance. Early Sunday morning, and the road was empty, the sun splashing against the blacktop and trees. Already, the leaves were beginning to turn, dull yellow and brick red interspersed with muted green. Thick trees gave way to farm-land—acres of yellowing cornstalks stretching as far as the eye could see. It reminded Malone of home. Or of what home had once been. The farm his grandfather had worked, that his father and uncle had taken over. Now his brothers and

cousins ran it, plowing and planting and harvest-
ing the way the family had done for generations.

Granddad would be proud.

Malone was, too. His siblings had turned
out well. His cousins were doing great. Malone
would like to think that he'd had something to
do with it. When he returned to the farm, he
always felt as if he was going home, and being
with his family always reminded him that the
things that mattered most were often the things
that were easiest to neglect.

He touched his scar, the corded flesh a harsh
reminder of just how quickly things could
change and just how quickly they could be lost.
He was supposed to be sitting in his kayak, con-
templating that and making decisions about just
where he planned to go with his life.

Quinn shifted, her hair brushing his neck, the
locks silky and soft. A widow at a very young
age. She hadn't said how her husband died, and
he hadn't asked. The question seemed too in-
timate, but he wanted to know. That surprised
him. He'd spent the past few years going from
one mission to another. He hadn't spent a lot of
time getting to know the people he was rescu-
ing. He hadn't thought it was necessary.

His grandfather would have corrected that assumption. He'd have said that investing in other

people's lives was always important, getting to know them always mattered.

The thing was, there was a lot more to living than completing missions. Malone had always known that, but the last few years, he'd lost sight of the truth.

That's what the life he'd been living had done to him. It had turned him into someone who only asked questions when it was necessary. It had changed him into a person who didn't know a whole lot about small talk or normal life.

Or maybe his military experience had done that. Losing his buddies, watching them die while he survived, had made him crave escape like other people craved ice cream. He took mission after mission because of that, assignment after assignment to keep himself from thinking about it too much.

A month ago, Chance had told him he was going to reach the finish line full speed, look back and realize that he'd been sprinting through a million blessings that he'd never even noticed.

That's what the vacation had been about— seeing the blessings instead of just the racetrack.

"I think that's it," August said, gesturing to an old house that stood at the back edge of open land, a huge decaying barn a few acres behind it. White clapboard siding stained gray with age, boarded-up windows, dry tangled grass: the place looked as if it had been abandoned decades ago. A crumbling driveway had once cut through the front yard. Now it was overgrown with withered dandelion stems and sharp-bladed brown grass.

August turned onto it, the bumping jolt of going from pavement to grass waking Quinn. She straightened, her cheeks still pink from sleep, her hair falling wild around her face.

"Please," she muttered, "tell me that I wasn't sleeping on your shoulder."

"I'd like to, but it would be a lie."

"Great. Perfect. Another thing to add to my list."

"What list?"

"Things that have made this day stink. I'm keeping it right next to my list of things that made my day great."

"You have a list of things that made your day great?"

"Of course."

"Maybe I should rephrase that—you actually have things that made today great?"

"I saw my brother for the first time in a couple years. I met some interesting people who seem determined to help me with a problem. I also… Actually, that may be it. I'd probably have more, but I've been a little distracted running for my life."

"A little?"

"A lot. Where are we, by the way?"

"Central Pennsylvania."

"At a house that looks like it's been abandoned. I'm assuming there's a reason for that. Other than we need to make a pit stop."

"Your brother needed medical attention," Chance offered. "We're pulling over to make sure he gets it."

"Pulling over at a hospital might be a better idea." She leaned over the seat and pulled up her brother's sleeve, revealing a deep gouge in his bicep, the wound seeping blood. "You're going to need stitches."

"It's not on my schedule for the day."

"Is a raging infection on your schedule for tomorrow?"

"No infection would dare show its face after Stella dressed a cut," Malone interrupted. "She's a former military nurse. She knows how to triage a wound."

She also knew how to show up where she was supposed to be, and she should be on the property. Malone didn't see any sign of Quinn's Jeep. "Has she texted you again, Chance?"

"The last text said she didn't know why we were taking so long."

"Sounds like Stella."

"Yeah, but this isn't like her. She should be

here." Chance scanned the area. "Can you drive this around to the back of the house?"

"Sure." August accelerated through a patch of grass, the SUV kicking up a cloud of dust. When it finally cleared, they'd come to a stop in a desolate yard—rusted swing set, dried-out plants, a garden area filled with choked weeds.

Still no sign of the Jeep.

"You're sure this is the right place," August asked, turning off the engine and opening his door. He'd lost a lot of blood, the bandage beneath his shirt now soaked with it.

Chance frowned, scrolling back through the texts. "She said an old boarded-up house with a crumbling barn behind it. First one we'd see."

"This has to be it then." Malone climbed out of the vehicle, that feeling sweeping over him again—the one that said danger, be on your guard, trouble ahead. His skin felt tight, the hair on his nape standing on end.

Nothing moved in the cornfield behind the house. No birds. No squirrels. No rabbits scurrying through the abandoned garden. The world had gone still, and he stilled, too, listening to the silence, to the soft swish of grass in the September breeze. He could feel rain in the air, smell rich loamy earth and decay.

Quinn grabbed his hand, her fingers warm and dry, her skin soft as she tried to pull him into the vehicle. "You guys need to get back in the car. Something's wrong."

No one responded. Chance had exited the vehicle, and he closed the door with a quiet snap that sent a lone bird flying from a gnarled oak. It cawed raucously, the sound sending a chill of warning through Malone's blood.

He stepped away from the SUV, motioning for August to move into position to block Quinn. She'd try to follow. He could almost guarantee that.

Chance moved in beside him, matching his pace as they headed toward the cornfield. It was the only place a Jeep could be hidden on the property. Everything else was too bare, too open.

"We'll split. You head east. I'll go west. Look for tire tracks. You find them, signal. We'll move in together." Chance split to the west, and Malone skirted around the edges of the cornfield.

No tracks. No sign that anyone had been there.

Stella was smart, though. She wouldn't have wanted to leave a trail.

He surveyed the property, looking for signs that she'd taken another route. In the distance, a road bisected the property. He could see just a hint of it, the blacktop gleaming in the sun. Had she used that as her access point?

He reached the edge of the cornfield, his gaze tracking the trajectory of the road. It curved around the property—first north and then west. If Stella had entered the property that way, she'd have ended up at the back of the cornfield, driving across grass and dirt to reach the house.

Unless the house wasn't where she'd been heading.

The old barn was at the back of the field, jutting up toward the blue sky, its brown-gray boards sagging, its roof caved in. He moved toward it, finally catching glimpse of what he was looking for—tire marks. They cut deep into the earth, revealing dark soil and bits of gravel. He followed the tracks to the double-wide doors of the barn. They yawned open, the floor of the barn littered with hay and abandoned farm equipment. No Jeep, but he could see that the other side of the barn dumped out into the cornfield—only a stretch of three or four hundred feet between it and the first stalks.

Had Stella gone there?

If she had, why?

A soft whistle broke the eerie silence. He whistled back, signaling for Chance to come to him. They'd done this kind of thing hundreds of times before—reconnaissance of an area, the two of them moving in sync as they surveyed a building, a piece of property and, now, an old barn.

Seconds later, Chance appeared in the barn doorway, his face grim. They didn't speak, just moved through side by side, exiting at the far end, stepping out into bright sunlight and the subtle scent of smoke.

"Where's that coming from?" Chance said, breaking the silence. There was no panic in his voice. There never was.

"I don't…" His voice trailed off as a plume of smoke snaked up from the western edge of the field. "There," he pointed, but Chance had already seen it.

"That can't be coincidental."

"Neither can that," Malone said, pointing to another plume, this one billowing up from the area he'd just walked. "They're flushing her out."

"Stella?"

"Who else could it be? I'm going in. You go back to the house."

"We're both going in. August knows how to take care of himself and his sister." He hoped, because he'd made keeping Quinn safe his business, and he never backed down once he made up his mind to do something.

Chance darted into the cornfield, following

a trail of broken and smashed stalks. Smoke snaked through the plants, curling up toward the sky in twirling black fingers. Malone could see flames eating along the plants a hundred yards away, the blaze moving rapidly.

Not good.

Chance had to know it, but he was plunging forward anyway, his focus on the tracks and whatever he was hoping to find at the end of them.

Stella alive. Unhurt.

That was the goal, but she'd never gone radio silent for this long. Not without forewarning.

"There!" Chance shouted, his voice hoarse from smoke and running, and Malone could see it—the Jeep, surrounded by corn stalks, the driver's door open.

"Stella!" he shouted, racing toward the vehicle a step behind his boss. Her purse was on the seat, her cell phone lying on the ground near the open door. Chance grabbed the purse, checking its contents. "Firearm is missing."

Malone snatched up the cell phone, saw an unsent message, partially written. Blue Toyota Camry has passed the house twi

"Looks like she spotted someone and planned to send you a text. She got interrupted."

"And now she's somewhere in this mess," Chance muttered. "Go back to the house," he continued. "Get August and Quinn out. I'll contact you when I have Stella."

He plunged into the cornstalks, fighting his way through tangled plant growth.

Malone could have let him go. Chance was smart, driven and tough, but he was acting on emotion, and that could get a person killed. Malone grabbed the back of his jacket, yanking him to a stop.

"Don't be a fool, Chance. There's no way you're going to find her by—"

"I won't if I keep standing here discussing it with you," Chance spat.

"You won't find her by running off without a plan," he finished, his words as calm as he could make them.

"I have a plan. You go. I'll stay." He jerked away, angrier than Malone had ever seen him. "That's a direct order, Malone. You disobey it, and you're off the team."

"Then I guess I'm off the team, because I'm not leaving you to burn to death in this mess," he responded, following Chance deeper into the cornfield, fire snapping at their heels.

SIX

Thick and acrid smoke filled Quinn's nose as she ran toward the burning cornfield. Malone was in there. So was Chance.

"What do you think you're doing?" August growled, grabbing her shoulder, spinning her around so rapidly she almost toppled.

"Going after Malone and Chance."

"They're smart. They'll find their way out. When they do, we're not going to be the reason they run back in."

She knew he was right.

She'd had dozens of firefighters in her classrooms over the years, teaching kids about fire safety. Never go back into the house. Your parents will find you outside.

Never go back in for a pet.

A toy.

A man who'd saved your life?

She'd do that, because she couldn't sit around hoping for the best.

She tried to yank out of her brother's hold, but he had a grip like steel. He shoved her into the backseat of the SUV, slamming the door before she could right herself.

"Don't move," he ordered as he opened the driver's door and climbed in. "You get out of this vehicle again, and I'll truss you up like a Thanksgiving turkey and stuff you in the trunk."

"There is no trunk," she snapped, her attention on the cornfield, the fire that was consuming it. First just black smoke. Then orange flames.

Where were they?

Shouldn't they be racing around the corner of the field by now? Sprinting toward the SUV, shouting that August needed to drive?

"They should be out of there by now," she said, the panic spilling out into the words. She could hear it, could feel her pulse thrumming through her veins.

She reached for the handle, because she could not sit and wait while two men were burned alive.

"I told you not to move!" August growled, the voice and tone one she'd never heard before.

"We can't just sit here."

He turned in his seat, his eyes blazing. "Do you think this is what I want? That I want to sit in this vehicle and stay safe while other men put their lives on the line? I want in there, but you are my first priority. Everyone else is second."

"Then, you go. I'll stay. I promise. I won't get out of this vehicle." Anything to offer help to Malone and Chance.

"And what if whoever set the fires finds you sitting here?"

She hadn't thought about it. She hadn't even considered that the fires had been set, that someone was out there, probably lying in wait. "I…don't know."

"Exactly. You don't have a weapon. Even if I left you with my handgun, you don't know how to fire it. You're helpless, Quinn. Just like Mom always was."

It was a jab out of left field.

"I'm not like our mother."

"Yeah. You are." He glanced in her direction, his dark gray eyes nearly black with emotion. "You care too much. You put everyone else first. You'd die before you let anyone you love be hurt."

"There's nothing wrong with that."

"There will be if you die, Quinn. Do you not understand that, either? I love you. You're my kid sister. I'm not going to sit back and watch you be hurt. Stay in the vehicle." He got out. Slammed the door.

She sat where she was, because she didn't know what else to do.

If she got out, she'd be putting everyone else in danger. If she stayed, she'd feel exactly like what August had said she was—helpless.

Her door flew open, and August was there.

"Scoot in!" he shouted, and she moved, sliding into the center seat as a red-haired woman dashed toward her. She was in the seat with the door closed so quickly that Quinn barely had time to blink.

"Stella. Silverstone," the woman panted, black soot smudged across one cheek, a bloody scratch on her hand. "Where are Chance and Malone?"

"Looking for you."

"Your friend—"

"Brother."

"Yeah. Him," she said impatiently. "Is texting them. Hopefully, they're not so idiotic that they're in the middle of that burning mess." The words were terse, but she was worried, Quinn could see it in her eyes.

"What happened?"

"Someone found me. I don't know how, but I plan to find out. Did your sister leave anything in the car before she left the kid? A cell phone maybe? Something that she could be tracked with?"

"No."

"Well, your car was being tracked. I know I wasn't followed, but someone knew exactly where I was." She wiped at the blood, muttering something under her breath that Quinn couldn't hear.

"What?"

"My first-aid kit is in my bag in a car that is about to be destroyed." Her gaze was on the cornfield, the flames that swept across it.

"That car is my Jeep," Quinn reminded her, and Stella sighed.

"I know. In retrospect, parking it in the middle of a fire hazard wasn't the best idea, but I was running out of time, and I needed cover. I'm sorry about it, though. I'll get you a new one when this is over."

Quinn would have laughed, if the situation weren't so deadly serious. "You can't just go and buy a Jeep for me, Stella. I have insurance. I'm sure it will cover—"

"Destruction by fire?" Stella said, a wry edge to her voice.

"Accidents happen."

"This was no accident. There were at least three men in that car. I got a look at one of them. I'd be happy to tell the police, but I think our best bet is to get out of here and contact the FBI."

"What—"

"There!" Stella cried, the relief in her voice and in her face undeniable. "Chance is out!"

She jumped from the SUV, racing toward a man who'd just stumbled out of the corn field. Quinn followed, praying that Malone would be next, that he'd sprint out from between corn stalks, run back toward the SUV.

He didn't, and she skidded to a stop next to Chance, her stomach churning with anxiety. "Where's Malone?"

"We saw someone. He went after him," he said, wiping a hand down his face, smearing the soot that covered every inch of his exposed skin.

"Why would you let him do something like that?" Stella demanded, pulling off her jacket and using it to swipe at his soot-coated face.

"I didn't," he replied, taking the jacket from her hand and finishing what she'd started.

"You're saying he defied your orders?"

"It's a long story, but if he doesn't get his…" His voice trailed off as someone crashed through the cornfield a few feet away. A man tumbled out. Not Malone. This guy had pale skin. Brown hair. A belly that hung over his belt. He had cuffs, too. On his wrists. And Malone, right behind him, looking mad as a hornet.

The guy stopped moving, and Malone gave him a not-so-gentle shove. "Keep going."

"You're going to be sorry for this," the guy

growled. "My boss..." He stopped himself. Shook his head. "You're going to be sorry."

"You're the one who looks sorry," Stella said, walking over and lifting his cuffed wrists. "Was the money your boss gave you worth going to jail for?"

"No way I'll be in jail. You'll see," he said belligerently. "I'll be out before the sun goes down, and you clowns are going to be sorry you ever messed with me."

"*Sorry* seems to be your favorite word," Malone said, his voice dangerously calm. "So, let's talk about other things that a person might be sorry for—like the fact that he was abandoned by his buddies?"

"They didn't abandon me. We all had different quadrants, and—"

"So, there were four of you, huh?" Malone nodded toward Chance, who typed something into his phone.

The guy pressed his lips together, and refused to answer.

Too late. He'd already let information slip out.

Malone eyed the cornfield and the smoke that billowed up from it. Quinn thought he might also be looking at the barn. It stood straight in the path of the fire.

"The smoke is pretty noticeable in a place like this. I wouldn't be surprised if someone called

911. We should be hearing sirens soon. You got some rope, August?" he asked. "We can tie this guy up in the barn and leave him for the police. Then we can get on with our day."

"That barn is going to go up like kindling!" the man protested, his gray-green eyes a little too small in his full face.

"So did the cornfield. While I was sitting in the middle of it." Stella took her jacket from Chance. "You can use this, Malone. Tie his legs. That'll keep him from going far."

"You can't leave me to burn to death!" The man pleaded, his eyes on the fire that was already lapping at the edges of the barn.

"Why not? Your friends did. Me? My buddies would never leave me behind. I'd never abandon them." Malone touched his scar, his eyes going dark for just a second. "The way I see things, if I had a comrade who was willing to risk his life for me, why wouldn't I risk mine for him?"

"You leave me there, and I'll die. That'll be murder!" the guy yelled.

"Seems to me, you have a real problem. Maybe you should think about how great your friends are while you're getting nice and toasty warm." He grabbed the guy by his arm, started dragging him toward the barn.

"Libby. Charles Libby," the guy shouted. "He's the one who got us all together and planned everything out. He had the money, and he got that from the boss."

"Who's the boss?" Malone asked, still dragging the guy along.

"I don't know!"

"Who are the other guys?"

"I don't know that, either."

"There's a lot you don't know, isn't there?"

"When someone offers money, I don't question it."

"Maybe you should." Malone shoved the man back toward the group, and he stumbled, stopping himself before he fell to his knees.

"It was supposed to be an easy job," the man said, his voice calmer. "Libby had already been tracking the kid through a device attached to her car seat."

The words chilled Quinn's blood, her mind spinning back to the moment when Tabitha had handed her the booster seat and the backpack.

Make sure she stays strapped in, Quinn. She's tiny for her age, and she can't be in a car without this.

Jarrod would have known that.

If he was as controlling, as mean, as abusive as Tabitha had said, than a tracking device on a booster seat made sense.

She shivered, realized that Malone was watching her, his eyes hooded, his face smeared with layers of soot. He looked hard and dangerous, and she was more glad than she'd ever been that he was on her side.

"Your sister was mistaken about who her husband would go after," Malone said. "He's not going after her. He wants Jubilee."

"To get at her?" she asked. "Tabitha seemed convinced that he didn't care about Jubilee. He didn't want her back."

"Someone wants her," the brown-haired guy said gleefully. "I got paid good money to make sure she was returned to wherever she's supposed to be."

"You planned on returning her after you burned her alive in a car?" Stella nearly spit the words out.

"We're not stupid. We knew the girl was taken somewhere and the car was being driven away from her. Libby figured you were trying to throw us off the track. No way was that going to happen. When the Jeep was driven in the cornfield, Libby said it might be a trap. We decided to flush the driver out and make her tell us where the girl was."

"That's a lot of work for a few thousand dollars," Chance said, his voice cold, his eyes icy blue.

"Hey, I have things I want. Easy money is easy money, and I take it where I can get it."

"What'd you spend it on?" August muttered. "A car? A fridge full of beer?"

"A down payment on a boat I've been wanting. Gonna do a little fishing and—"

"What you're going to do," Malone said, "is wish that you'd saved the money for bail. I hear sirens. Let's get this guy out front, so we can talk to the police and get on our way."

Chance grabbed the guy by the arm, manhandling him around the corner of the house, Stella right beside him. August mumbled something and followed, fresh blood rolling down his arm.

He needed medical attention. Quinn should have run after him, made sure that he got it, but her feet felt leaden, her mind numb.

She'd believed her sister.

After all the lies, the drugs, the cons she'd pulled, Quinn had still wanted to trust that Tabitha was telling the truth.

"Just because Tabitha was wrong, doesn't mean she lied," Malone said as if he knew exactly what she was thinking.

"The evidence is stacking up against her." She smoothed her hair, tried to keep her voice steady. "Besides, Tabitha has a history of being dishonest."

"I have a cousin who was like that." He dropped an arm around her shoulder, the weight of it familiar and comforting. Quinn had forgotten what it felt like to have a man's arm around her. She'd forgotten what it was like to walk side by side with someone.

She'd forgotten, and maybe she shouldn't have remembered, because it felt good. It felt nice. It felt, if she really thought about it, a lot like being home.

"Is she in jail?" she asked through the lump in her throat.

He laughed, the sound vibrating through her shoulder. "*He* is now a pastor. With five kids and a wife who adore him. People change, Quinn." He stopped, looked straight into her eyes. "All the time. Don't give up on your sister until you know for sure that she hasn't. Okay?"

She nodded, and he smiled. Not an open cheerful smile. A soft one that made something in her heart spring to life.

"Good. Now, how about we go make sure our perp tells the police everything he told us."

The thing about police was that they liked to be thorough. In small towns, like the one Malone and the team had found themselves stuck in, they were even more thorough.

He could understand that. Successful prosecution rested on their ability to process scenes and evidence properly. They often had to do it with a lower budget and fewer officers.

Yeah. He understood, and the deputy and sheriff who'd shown up in response to Chance's call were as professional as any law enforcement officer Malone had ever met. He'd have been able to appreciate that, if he hadn't been standing around twiddling his thumbs for an hour.

He glanced at his phone. No text from Boone. His connecting flight must have departed on time. Good news for Boone and for Jubilee. Agent Spellings had left a message after she'd heard from the local PD, and she'd assured Malone that they had Jubilee in protective custody. No one was going to get an opportunity to kidnap her. That was great.

What would have been greater would be the FBI bringing Jarrod Williams in for questioning.

That was currently out of the question. According to Spellings, there wasn't enough probable cause. Could be that was true, but Malone had been doing a little research while he was waiting for the local PD to finish. Jarrod Williams was a big deal in Las Vegas. He owned enough property to be a millionaire several times over. He had several businesses and investments and was currently making a bid for state senate.

A guy like that would have a lot to lose if he

went to jail. He'd have a lot to lose if people found out he was an abuser.

"You're deep in thought," Quinn said. She'd made herself comfortable on an old porch swing that hung from rusted chains. The thing looked as though it would fall if a feather landed on it, but the chains hadn't quit yet.

"What did your sister say about Jarrod?" he asked.

"That's what you were thinking about? Jarrod?" She rested her chin on her bent knees, the swing creaking as it moved. There were freckles on her nose and cheeks and her eyes seemed darker gray in the late-morning light. Slate rather than dove.

Pretty, but he wasn't sure why he was noticing.

His job required he spend time with all different kinds of people. Men. Women. Children. Ugly. Attractive. Mean. Nice. Bitter. Sweet. He'd never cared one way or another about those things. His job was to find the missing and to bring them home, and that's what he did.

Running the race but not noticing the scenery. He wanted to thank Chance for putting the thought in his head, because now he couldn't shake it.

"That and other things," he responded, stepping onto the porch and moving toward her.

She scooted over, patting the bench seat. "There's room."

"I'm not worried about room. I'm worried about weight limit."

She laughed, but there was tension in her face, tightness in her narrow shoulders. "My sister didn't say much about her husband. She said he was mean, that he had connections. That he could get her tossed into jail if he wanted to. Or have her silenced."

"Did she tell you he was running for senate?"

"She said he was rich, and that she liked the money and wealth and things marrying him brought. She also said…" She frowned, pinching the bridge of her nose, her eyes closing briefly. "I can't believe I forgot this."

"What?"

"She said something really odd when she was talking about Jarrod. She said, 'He was nice, handsome and generous. There wasn't any way I could resist that, and then when I met Jubilee, I was hooked for good.' Something like that anyway. It struck me for about three seconds, but I was so shocked to see her on my doorstep, I guess I didn't hold on to it very long."

"So, you think that Jarrod had Jubilee when he and Tabitha met?" The possibility intrigued Malone. Tabitha's description made Jarrod sound like someone who liked to be in control, someone who would insist that he be paid the utmost respect. He didn't sound like someone who would go out of his way to commit a crime that wouldn't benefit him. And what good would kidnapping Jubilee have done?

"I don't know. That's the way it sounds, though. Don't you think?"

"I think we need to talk to your sister *and* her husband."

"My sister is missing, and Las Vegas is a long way from here."

"We're going to find your sister, and I don't need to go to Las Vegas to talk to her husband. Stella is very good at getting information we need. I'll put her on it."

She nodded, standing and stretching, a ring on her right hand glinting in the sun. It caught his attention, the narrow gold band enough like a wedding ring for him to wonder if it was one.

Not his business, but his mouth opened anyway, and he was asking before he could stop himself. "Is that your wedding ring?"

She frowned, twisting the band. "Yes. People kept telling me to take it off, and move on, but I couldn't bring myself to not wear it, so I shifted it onto my right hand. I know it seems silly, but—"

"Why do you say that?"

"What?" She met his eyes, and he found himself caught in her gaze, noticing a dozen things that he hadn't seen before. The blue flecks in her eyes. The thickness of her lashes, and the way they brushed her cheeks when she blinked. The smoothness of her skin and the golden strands that seemed woven through her hair.

"That it seems silly to wear the ring."

"Because Cory has been gone for three years, and our marriage ended when he died."

"That doesn't mean you don't still love him."

She shrugged, twirling the ring once and then letting her hand drop. "No one tells you how to move on when someone you love dies or how to stop being the caregiver when the hospital bed that's sitting in your living room is finally empty."

"Was he sick for long?" he asked, imaging that empty bed in the empty room, imaging just how hard that would have been to face alone.

"In the grand scheme of our marriage? An eternity, but it was really only a year. He had brain cancer, and it took everything from him, and then it took everything from me." Her cheeks went bright pink, and she frowned. "That sounds really melodramatic."

"I don't think so. I think it sounds like how you feel."

"How I felt. Things are back on track now,

but I'm still not ready to take off the ring. Not yet, and I don't even really know why."

He thought he did.

He thought that maybe she couldn't quite let go of the dreams she'd had when she'd said her vows, that she didn't really want the good times she'd shared with her husband to be over.

He could understand that. He could also understand how difficult it would be to let go of forever, to know that a lifetime with someone had only amounted to a few short years.

"You know what I think, Quinn?" he asked, and she frowned.

"Do I want to?"

"Maybe. I think you should wear that ring for as long as you want to. I think you should never feel anything but happy to do it. You're honoring the memory of what you had with your husband. There's nothing wrong with that. Now, how about we find Chance? He's trying to talk the sheriff into letting us leave."

"I don't see why we shouldn't be able to."

"Have you looked around recently?" He gestured to the black field, the blackened exterior of her Jeep, the smoldering barn. Fire crews had put out the fire quickly, but not before property had been destroyed. "There's been a lot of damage done here today."

"We didn't do it."

"No, but they want to make sure that's the case. If they let us go and find out we were part of this, it will make their office look pretty foolish."

"What about the guy you handcuffed? Shouldn't he be their prime suspect?"

"His name is Anthony Gray. A small-time thug who is already wanted on a couple of outstanding warrants. He's already been booked for arson. The sheriff said he's singing like a jaybird, but he's not saying much more than he already told us."

"What he told us makes me really suspicious of my sister's husband. Who else would hire someone to kidnap Jubilee?"

"Good question," he responded, helping her down nearly rotted wood steps. "Let's go see what Chance has dug up."

"If he's dug up anything."

"Trust me. Chance can find out just about anything about anyone."

And Malone was eager to hear what he had to say about Jarrod. Quinn was right. Tabitha's husband was the only one who would have any motive for kidnapping Jubilee. Did he want the little girl back?

Or did he want to use her as a pawn to get to Tabitha?

They needed to find out, because until they understood his motive, they couldn't predict his next move.

SEVEN

There was something about Malone, something that Quinn couldn't deny or ignore. It made her want to tell him things she hadn't ever told anyone else. Things about Cory and their life together. About the way it had felt to lose him, to have to move on without the person she'd planned to move forward with. Things she'd never talked about because she didn't think anyone else could understand.

Heartache was such a private thing.

Grief was a journey a person could only ever take alone.

At least, that's what she'd always thought. In that first year after Cory's death, she'd had friends and church—people bringing meals and offering prayer and encouraging her to get out, live life. Eventually, people moved on and expected her to move on, too.

Malone seemed different.

He seemed to understand the depth of her

heartache. Maybe that came from living his own sorrows. She'd seen him touch his scar, and she'd known there was a story. One he wasn't ready to tell.

She glanced his way, saw that he was studying her, his dark eyes skimming her hair and her face, her soot-stained shirt and her filthy sneakers.

"What? Do I have soot on my face?" she asked, rubbing her palm down her cheek.

He shook his head. "Just thinking."

"About?"

"Running races without looking at the scenery.

"Is that code for something?"

"Maybe." He smiled, guiding her across the yard and to the SUV, his hand warm on the curve of her waist.

Chance was leaning against the vehicle, his phone to his ear, his gaze on Stella and August. They were head-to-head, looking at something on August's phone. Neither seemed to notice that she and Malone had returned.

Interesting.

August had dated someone seriously a few years back, but she'd wanted him to give up his job, live a more predictable and safe life. He'd refused. Of course. To August, his job was everything. It consumed him, made him difficult to reach and, sometimes, difficult to talk to. There were long stretches of time when Quinn didn't hear from him, when her phone calls went unanswered and her texts got ignored. Once, it had gone on so long, she'd hopped in her car and driven to his place. He'd been home, bleary-eyed from whatever job he'd just returned from. She'd made him dinner, stuck around for two nights and listened to him play sad tunes on his guitar. Finally, he'd snapped out of whatever place he'd been in. He'd cheered up, taken her out on a long hike and regaled her with amusing stories about his life. He'd seemed like his old self and she'd left knowing he was going to be all right.

She still worried about him. Seeing him with Stella gave her hope that he might find someone he could connect with, someone he could share his other stories with—the darker ones, the ones that he didn't want to tell Quinn.

Stella finally looked up, smiling as she tucked a strand of bright red hair behind her ear. She had a bandage wrapped around her palm, the gauze crisp white. August had fresh bandages as well, his sleeve cut away, his shoulder padded by gauze and tape.

"Did your first-aid kit survive the fire?" Quinn asked Stella.

"Nah. I borrowed one from the police. Who,

I might add, are taking their sweet time clearing us to leave."

"That's okay," Chance said, shoving his phone into his pocket. "Some of us put the time to good use."

"Some of us," Stella retorted, "aren't workhorses."

There was an undercurrent between the two, some unspoken feelings that pulsed through the air every time they looked in each other's eyes. Had they been a couple? If so, they didn't seem to have ended things well.

"Workhorses get things done, and they find out interesting facts."

"Like?" Malone asked.

"Jarrod Williams used to be affiliated with a cult that got shut down for running drugs and guns into the US from Mexico. At the time, he went by the name Jerry Cornwall. Guess he decided to change it once he left. I sent the information to Boone. If it's the same cult his ex was in, we may have a link between Jarrod and Jubilee that precedes Jubilee's relationship with Tabitha."

"Which means that Tabitha didn't kidnap Jubilee?" Quinn had doubted her sister's ability to do such a thing, and this seemed to support that doubt.

"At this point, I'm not sure what it means. It's

possible your sister and Jarrod met in the cult and reconnected a couple of years later. It's also possible that Jarrod was in the cult, met Jubilee's mother and somehow ended up with the kid. I've passed the information to law enforcement. They're digging deeper."

"It seems to me," Malone said, "that the police have probable cause to bring Williams in for questioning."

"Probable cause for what crime?" Chance sighed, raking his fingers through thick chestnut hair. "If Boone's ex handed the kid over, Williams has been raising her like his own because he was asked to. The FBI plans to question him when he returns from overseas, but—"

"Are they sure he's out of country?" Stella cut in.

"He boarded a plane in Las Vegas, landed in Baltimore and boarded a flight for London a few hours later. That's all verified. He's expected to return Wednesday."

"He's got plenty of money. It seems to me," Malone said, "that he could have had someone take his place on the outward-bound flight to London. All he had to do was pay someone to buy a ticket, have them go through security and meet near the gate. They exchange boarding passes and the stand-in boards the flight."

"That's a lot of effort to get back at his wife,"

August pointed out. "Especially when he could have hired someone to take care of things while he was gone, made sure his alibi was airtight. If the FBI is suspicious enough, they can pull security footage to verify his presence on the plane. There are cameras all over the airports."

Malone shrugged, his broad shoulders pulling the fabric of his T-shirt taut. "It might not be about getting back at his wife. We've been focused on the kid, the things Tabitha supposedly stole. But Jarrod Williams isn't who he's pretending to be. The fact that he's changed his name at least once, been involved in an organization that was breaking the law, is a good indication that he has things to hide. What if Tabitha knew some of those things? What if she ran because she was afraid?"

"And made him afraid?" Quinn hadn't thought about that. Her sister was good at conning people. She knew how to work a mark and how to get what she wanted. She'd have recognized underhanded dealings, and she'd have known Jarrod was a fake.

Knowing her, she wouldn't have cared.

Money was everything.

Until Jubilee became part of her life? Had nurturing the little girl made her want to clean up her act, get things right?

That's what Quinn wanted to think.

Only Tabitha knew for sure.

Tabitha…

Was she okay? Hurt? Alive?

She shuddered, the thought of her sister lying somewhere injured—or worse—filling her with dread.

"If she knows something that he doesn't want anyone else to find out, then yes," Malone said quietly, his hand sweeping up her arm and settling on her shoulder. "We'll find her, and we'll figure it all out."

"The best way to do that," Stella remarked, her short hair springing in a hundred different directions, "is to find that husband of hers. Every word anyone says seems to lead us in that direction. Anyone have his phone number? I might be able to get a handle on where he is. Or, at least, how soon he can be in the New England area."

"How—?" Quinn started to say, but Chance was already rattling off a number that he said he'd gotten from a friend who worked for Las Vegas police, and Stella was punching it into her phone. She waited while it rang, a satisfied smile on her face.

Jarrod's voice mail must have picked up, because Stella left a short message about being a real estate developer in Boston and wanting to break into the Las Vegas market. She said she'd been following Jarrod's career and was intrigued. She'd put up three-quarters of the capital for a fifty-fifty partnership. All he had to do was find the right project. She left a name—not hers. A couple of numbers. Ended the call, the satisfied smile still on her face.

"That should do it. If he's as keen on money and prestige as everyone seems to think, it won't take long for him to call me back."

"Don't you think he'll check out your story first?" August frowned. "The guy knows the police and FBI are investigating. He's got to know that they're checking out his story."

"I gave him the name of a friend who is a real estate developer in Boston. She's a navy buddy." She typed a text message as she spoke, sent it, her smile broadening. "And, now she's been informed. She'll play along. If he calls her office, she's going to claim to be my assistant and direct him to my cell phone number. I do love when things work out." She sighed happily. "Now, how about we find the police and get cleared to leave? I've got a hot date next weekend, and I want to be well rested for it."

She strode off, her hair gleaming in the sunlight, her jeans black from smoke.

"Wow," Quinn murmured.

"Yeah," Malone responded, his breath ruffling her hair, his hand still warm on her shoulder. "She's something."

"She's what I want to be when I grow up," Quinn responded. The confidence. The assertiveness. The ability to solve problems. Those were things she was constantly striving for and wasn't sure she'd ever achieve.

"No," Malone said. Just that one word, and she met his eyes, looked long enough to see hints of gold in the deep brown irises. He had stunning eyes, thick lashes, and that scar that seemed to only add to his tough good looks.

"No what?" she asked.

"No, you don't want to grow up to be Stella, because that would mean not growing up to be you, and I kind of like the you I've gotten to know. Looks like the police cleared us." His hand slipped away from her shoulder, and he gestured to Stella who was running toward them, a pink backpack dangling over her arm, her free hand waving wildly.

"They've cleared us to go," she called. "Let's get out of here while the getting is good! This yours or the kid's?" She shoved the backpack into Quinn's arms.

"Jubilee's. I should have given it to CPS. I wasn't thinking clearly."

"Did you look in it?" Malone asked, taking the pack from her hands.

"Yes. My sister's priorities are different than mine. Either that or she let Jubilee pack. There are a couple of stuffed animals, a few books and a change of clothes." There'd been a small photo album, too. Pictures of Jubilee and a man who must have been Jarrod. Photos of Christmas gifts and birthday parties. One page had a Post-it note with Quinn's name scribbled across the front of it. She'd only had time to glance at the picture of a man who'd looked a few decades older than Jarrod and Tabitha. A friend of theirs? One of Jarrod's parents? She'd had no idea, and she'd been in too much of a rush to take it out of the album and look more closely.

"Not much seeing as how the kid was leaving home for good."

"I know."

"Get in!" Stella demanded, gunning the engine for emphasis.

In seconds, they were on the road, speeding north toward Maine. Hopefully, they could follow Tabitha's trail from there.

"I wonder if Agent Spellings is done with my phone, and if there were any more phone calls while she had it?" she said aloud. "If Tabitha is in danger—"

"I got a call about that, sis," August interrupted. "Sorry. So much happened I forgot to tell you. They've determined that the scream was dubbed. They also found the phone."

"Where?"

"Dropped in a trash can just outside of Echo Lake. They dusted for prints. Found Tabitha's and an unknown set. Probably the guy who made the call."

"No sign of Tabitha, though? Did they see any of her clothes? Her purse?" Quinn could imagine her sister, tied up and gagged, lying somewhere alone.

Please, God, let her be okay.

The silent prayer filled her mind, and she wondered if she'd get the answer she wanted. Something more than the no she'd received when she'd begged for Cory to be healed.

God's ways are best. That's what all her friends had said, but it didn't feel best when someone you loved was sick and hurting and God didn't provide the healing they so desperately needed.

"Quinn," August said. "You need to stop worrying about Tabitha. She's fine. She staged this whole thing so that the police would point fingers at her husband and forget that she stole hundreds of thousands of dollars' worth of cash and jewelry."

"Seems pretty far-fetched to me." Malone shifted, his thigh brushing against Quinn's leg. Somehow she'd ended up between him and Chance again.

"What?" August asked. "That my lying con woman of a sister would lie and con the most naive and easily tricked—"

"How about you stop?" Malone said. "Before you say something you are going to regret."

"What I'm saying is the truth. Quinn has always been—"

"Smart," Malone interjected. "She believes Tabitha is in danger. Until we have evidence to support that, we'll act on her assumption."

"You don't have to stand up for me, Malone. I'm perfectly capable of doing it myself."

"Just because you *can* do something alone, doesn't mean you have to," he responded.

"If Tabitha's phone has been found," Stella said, "are the police taking the threat against her any more seriously?"

The question was directed toward August, and Quinn was interested in the answer.

"Agent Spellings is great at saying that she's looking into things when she doesn't want to directly answer a question," he responded, shifting in his seat and meeting Quinn's eyes. "I'm sorry, kid. There's bad blood between me and Tabitha, but it has nothing to do with you. I shouldn't let it influence the way I act. If you think that she's in danger, I'm willing to go along with it."

"It's—"

Before she could finish, Chance's cell phone buzzed. He glanced at the screen. Frowned. "My sister Charity has been watching local Echo Lake news. She works for HEART, and helps us keep track of events in the locations where we're working. There's been a body found in the water. Local PD is on the scene."

"Male or female?" Quinn said, her body icy with fear, her throat tight with it.

"No news on that, yet. She called but local PD won't answer questions."

"So, it could be Tabitha." The words echoed through the silent car.

No one responded.

Quinn guessed that they had no idea what to say.

Seven hours, one stop for gas and a few terse conversations, and they were riding through what looked to Malone like a Norman Rockwell painting—well-lit houses on quiet streets, old Victorian homes standing on distant hills, water gleaming in the moonlight.

Stella pulled up in front of a row of brownstones—the pretty brick buildings nestled one right next to the other, their pitched roofs and dormered attics quaint and charming. Five shops were housed in the buildings, their door signs turned to Closed probably hours ago. It was a nice street in the business district of a small town. Malone imagined it got very quiet at night, and very lonely for anyone who might be renting space above one of the shops.

Anyone like Quinn.

Sure, the crime rate was probably nil, but being alone made a person an easy target. Especially if that person was young, female and attractive.

Stella parked, and he got out of the SUV. Here, the air held more than a hint of fall, the coolness of it bathing his face as he offered Quinn a hand.

"Finally home," he said, and she nodded, climbing out of the vehicle.

She seemed steady enough, okay enough, but she'd been quiet during the trip, all her usual questions and speculations kept to herself.

She was worried about her sister.

He couldn't blame her. They still hadn't been given information about the body. Agent Spellings hadn't returned calls, and Charity hadn't been able to dig up any further information. The police were keeping quiet, the medical examiner was mum, all they knew for certain was that a body had been pulled from the lake.

"I'll let you guys in, and then I'm going to the sheriff's office. I know him from church. He'll tell me what I want to know." She jogged past him, racing up metal stairs that stretched up the side of the last building in the row.

He followed, grabbing her hand before she could unlock the door. "Careful," he cautioned.

"Of what?"

"You're deep into this now, Quinn. Anything could happen." He took the keys, the metal staircase clanging as the rest of the group ascended. "Let me check things out before you go in."

The door creaked open before he inserted the key, and he gestured for Chance and Stella to move in. August followed behind them.

"What's going on?" Quinn whispered as if talking loudly would bring danger down on their heads.

He ignored the question, easing the door farther open as Stella hit the landing and positioned herself behind him.

"Door was unlocked," he said quietly and felt her nod as he cleared the threshold and walked into a dark living room.

He knew something was wrong before he turned on the light. A table had been upended, pillows lay on the floor. He ran his hand along the wall, flicked on the light.

Trashed.

That was the best way to describe it.

Cushions slashed, books torn off shelves. Damp splotches on the carpet. A porcelain lamp lay shattered next to the fireplace.

He pulled his gun, heard Quinn gasp. Stella would keep her out. Chance would call the police. Malone was going to search the place, make sure it was as empty as it seemed, see if there was any sign that Tabitha had been there.

What better place for her to hide out?

From August's description, she was street-smart and savvy. She knew how to work a situation to her advantage. She'd have known that Quinn's apartment would be empty for a night or two. Why not break in? Sleep? Maybe take a few things she needed for whatever trip she planned to take?

He moved through the living room, eased into a narrow hall. The place felt empty but he wasn't taking any chances.

There were three doors there. All opened. A bathroom. Empty. Office with futon and desk covered with knickknacks that had probably come from students. Also empty. None of the areas had been touched. No drawers pulled out. No cabinets emptied.

Whoever had trashed the living room hadn't bothered there.

He walked to the final room, peering into a large space.

Like the living room, it had been wrecked. Sheets and blankets on the floor. Books thrown. A Bible lay spine up a few feet from the door, the pages fanned out and crinkled.

The floor creaked as Malone moved to a closet door. He opened it, found nothing but gauzy dresses and a few pairs of shoes. He turned, scanning the room, his gaze settling on the floor on the far side of the bed, the purse that lay beside it—contents dumped, money spilling out. Lots of money. More than he thought Quinn would ever carry around.

A splotch of red stained the wood floor a few feet away from it, and Malone crouched near it, studying what looked like blood. There was another splotch a few inches away. One on the white sheet that lay at the foot of the bed.

The mirror on the dresser had a crack in it, a bronze globe lying dented beside it.

The place hadn't just been trashed. There'd been a fight there. A violent one. Based on the spots of blood on the floor and the bedding, someone had been hurt.

Tabitha and someone else?

He moved to the window. It looked out over an empty lot dotted with dry grass and spare plants. A few trees marked the edge of the property, and beyond those, several trees towered up toward the night sky. He could see the lake through them, the water gleaming with reflected moonlight.

A pretty view, but the lake and the empty lot made undetected access to the brownstones easy. All a person had to do was walk along the shoreline, cross the empty lot, pick a lock and enter the building.

"Malone?" Quinn called, her voice shaky.

Stella should have held her back, but she was there, in the doorway, her eyes wide. "What happened in here?"

"To me, it looks like a fight." He tried to position himself so she couldn't see the purse, but she moved into the room, Stella right behind her, her face red with anger or embarrassment.

"I tried to stop her," she sputtered. "But she slipped right past me. I must be getting old. I've never had someone so puny get the better of me."

Malone would have laughed, but Quinn had spotted the purse.

She crouched next to the dumped bag.

"Don't touch it," he warned, stooping beside her, scanning the items that lay on the floor— wallet, keys, lipstick, money. A child's hair band, the glittery plastic ends of it something no adult would ever wear.

"It's Tabitha's," Quinn said, her face parchment pale. "She must have come back here after I left."

"She might have thought it was a safe place to stay," Stella said gently. She must have suddenly realized what she was seeing, what it meant.

"It wasn't, though." Quinn pointed to the red stains. "That's blood. She was attacked here. The body in the lake—"

"Just because she was attacked, doesn't mean she's dead." Things looked bad. That was true, but Malone had seen a lot of things during his career. Not all of them were what they seemed.

"It doesn't mean she's alive, either," Quinn said, her gaze still focused on the purse. "Someone's body was in the lake, and all my sister's stuff is here. She's not." Her voice broke, and he pulled her to her feet.

"Are August and Chance still on the landing?" he asked, wanting to distract her from the purse, the body, her thoughts about her sister.

"Yes."

"Go tell them that we need the police here quickly. Chance knows how to get the local PD moving fast. He can do it a lot more efficiently than I can." That wasn't quite the truth. They were all good at getting people to respond the way they wanted. It was part of the job—

making sure local authorities were willing and happy to cooperate with the mission.

Quinn probably knew it. She hesitated, her gaze dropping to the purse again before she nodded.

"I'll tell them," she said, and then she nearly ran from the room.

EIGHT

The body wasn't Tabitha's.

That was what Quinn had wanted to know, and Sheriff Cameron Lock was quick to assure her that the deceased was a middle-aged man. Probably a drifter who'd had too much to drink and fallen in the lake. An autopsy had been scheduled, but as far the sheriff was concerned, there was no connection between the dead man and Tabitha.

Good. Great.

Quinn was happy to hear it. The problem was, Tabitha was still missing, and Quinn was sitting in an SUV waiting for the police to finish collecting evidence in her apartment.

DNA evidence. Fingerprints. Photos. They'd called in the state crime lab to oversee things. They were being cautious and careful. Which was exactly what Quinn wanted, but she also wanted to be done. Normally, Quinn thought of herself as a patient person. Right then, she felt anything but able to wait things out.

She had to find Tabitha.

Had to.

And sitting in the SUV wasn't going to help her do that.

It also wasn't going to help her explain who'd broken into her apartment, whose blood was on her floor, if that person was still alive.

Quinn had a feeling that her sister was the answer to the first question. She hoped she wasn't the answer to the second. As far as the third went, Malone kept assuring her that there was every chance, every hope that her sister was still alive.

She wasn't even sure she knew how to hope anymore.

She'd tried. She prayed, she read her Bible, she offered her petitions up to God. In the end, she felt as empty as she had the day Cory had told her he was done with treatment, that all he wanted was a few more months of peace and happiness.

She pushed away the thought.

That situation had been different.

This one couldn't be nearly as hopeless. She couldn't be nearly as helpless as she'd felt then. She didn't have to sit around waiting for other people to offer her hope. She could go out and find reasons to hope herself.

She shifted in her seat, eyeing the facade of the brownstone that housed her apartment. She'd loved the place the minute she'd seen it. The two bedroom, one bath space above a bakery had been the perfect place for a newly widowed woman. There'd been hardwood and old plaster walls. Pretty medallion ceilings in the living area and an oversize 1920s stove in the kitchen. More than anywhere she'd ever lived, it had felt like home.

The day she'd moved in, she'd cried thinking about Cory, about what she'd thought they'd have together—the lifetime they'd planned. She'd cried, and then she'd unpacked and she'd started her new life, because that had been the only thing that made sense for her to do. She'd always been a person of action. She'd always done what needed to be done to achieve her dreams and accomplish her goals.

So, why was she sitting there like a lump while other people solved her problems?

"Enough," she muttered, opening the door and stepping out into the cold night air. Her sweatshirt had disappeared after the fire, and she shivered as the coolness seeped through her T-shirt. There was nothing she could do in the apartment, but the local diner was open, and she knew the people there would tell her everything they'd heard about the man who'd died. Even better, if Tabitha had been in to eat, they'd remember her. They'd be able to tell Quinn how her sister had looked, how she'd acted.

If she'd been there.

She thought about checking in with August or Malone. She could see the two men deep in discussion with several sheriff's deputies. The break-in at Quinn's apartment was big news in a town like this, and the sheriff and most of his deputies had responded to the call.

Quinn knew most of them by name. She could have called out to any of them, announced her plans and headed out, but she'd walked to the diner alone dozens of times before. She knew the way like the back of her hand—knew the well-lit sidewalk along Main Street, the tiny side road that connected to 5th Avenue.

The place wasn't far, an easy walk, and she needed some air, some exercise and some time to think. Besides, Echo Lake was safe, the crime rate so low she wasn't even sure it existed.

She hitched her purse onto her shoulder and walked east, bypassing a long row of brownstones that had once been private homes but were now businesses—a chocolate shop, a bakery, a used bookstore, a yarn store. She'd always enjoyed the quaintness of her adopted hometown—the well-kept properties, the kind and sometimes nosey residents. Cory had grown up there, and he'd wanted to return after college. She'd wanted to make him happy so she'd agreed.

She hadn't thought that she'd fall in love with the area, but she had. Now, years later, she couldn't imagine living anywhere else.

She crossed Main Street, turned onto Piper Way.

This street was darker, no businesses with exterior lights—just a couple of empty lots and a church that had seen better days, the old clapboard siding hanging this way and that, the windows coated with years' worth of grime. It had been at least a decade since the church had been occupied, the old location giving way to a newer, bigger building on a more upscale, touristy street. She'd heard rumors that someone was purchasing the old church and turning it into a youth center.

She hoped so. Even with the cemetery behind it—headstones dotting a grassy knoll that overlooked the town—the building was charming.

A pebble bounced across the street in front of her, and she stopped, her heart pounding frantically. Moonlight danced through the breeze-swaying trees and dotted the grass and pavement with golden light. No one had bothered putting street lights on the road, but she could see the old church fence, the steps that led up to its door. She could see the cemetery behind it, the whitish stones visible through the darkness.

Shadows swayed on the road in front of her, blocking her path to 5th Avenue. She'd never been afraid to walk across that darkest patch of road. She'd never worried about the tall pine tree that hid her view of the well-lit street beyond. Her pulse slushed in her ears, her skin cold with fear.

"Quinn," she thought she heard someone whisper, the name mixing with the swish of grass in the breeze, the rustle of leaves.

Behind her, another pebble skipped across the road, and she whirled, her heart in her throat. Was someone in the shadows by the corner of the church? She peered in the darkness, eyes probing the blackest areas.

"Quinn," that whisper again, and this time she was certain it was her name.

"Who is it?" she called, her voice shaking.

"Me, dummy! Hurry up, before they find us."

Tabitha.

Relief flooded over her, and she didn't think, just darted off the sidewalk and into the churchyard.

Someone grabbed her, a rough hand covering her mouth as she was dragged toward the trees. She heard someone screaming, the sound piercing through a haze of panic. Tabitha? Did they have her, too?

She fought, ripping the hand away from her mouth, screaming. The sound was cut off by that hand, slamming over her face, covering her mouth. Her nose.

"Shut up and stop fighting!" a man growled, his free arm hooking around her neck, pressing against her jugular. "Or I will kill you."

She could hear the desperation in his voice, and she knew he'd do it.

She stilled and the pressure on her throat eased.

"Call your sister!" he demanded.

"What?"

"Call her name!"

"No."

He spun her around, slapped her so hard she saw stars.

"Do you want to die tonight?" he snarled, his eyes gleaming in the darkness. "Call your sister! Yell for help. She's close. I heard her talking to you."

Quinn wasn't going to do it, and she braced herself for another blow.

Something moved in the trees behind her attacker, leaves swaying soundlessly, a shadow moving silently between thick pine boughs.

Tabitha?

No. The person was broader, taller, moving stealthily, not even a hint of hesitation. A man? She thought so, but it was too dark to see, and then she was slapped again, the blow knocking her off her feet.

She fell hard, the breath knocked from her lungs, her vision going dark. She heard grass and leaves crackling, the sound of two bodies colliding. A man called out. A woman responded. And, then her vision cleared, and she could see shadowy forms milling around her. One. Two. Three.

A guy on the ground, Malone standing over him, a knee in his back.

"Get up," he growled, yanking the man to his feet, and shoving him toward a deputy. "You want to take care of him?"

He didn't wait for an answer, just crouched beside Quinn, his expression unreadable in the darkness. "That wasn't the smartest move you've ever made, Quinn," he said, his arm slipping around her waist.

"I didn't think—"

"Obviously not!" August snapped. "You could have been killed."

She didn't respond.

He was right.

She'd taken a stupid chance.

She just hadn't realized it was stupid at the time.

"Echo Lake has always been safe. I've walked to the diner dozens of times," she tried to explain, but August raised his hand, cutting her off.

"This isn't dozens of times, sis. This is tonight, and we're dealing with some dangerous people."

Who aren't after me, was on the tip of her tongue, but obviously they were. Obviously, they'd planned to use her to get to Tabitha.

"Tabitha—"

"Stella and Chance are going after her. We think she was in the church, but we got on the scene too late to see which direction she was headed when you were attacked." Malone touched Quinn's chin, tilting her head with his finger and leaning in close. "You're going to have some nice bruises."

"It's better than being dead," August muttered. "As for Tabitha. I can tell you one thing for sure, Quinn. She didn't run to your rescue. As a matter of fact, she took off running, and she didn't look back."

"She saw the cavalry," Malone pointed out.

"She knew help was here. It's not like she abandoned Quinn."

"It *is* like that, Malone," August retorted. "She dragged Quinn into her mess, and she's leaving her to deal with it. Typical in my family, but you'll figure that out yourself after a while. I'm going to see if I can find her. I'll try to think like a coward. That might help."

"Guess he's a little bitter," Malone said, his hand sliding from Quinn's side to her back.

"He was the oldest son. She was the oldest daughter. He tried to make things work in the family, she jumped ship." That was the simple explanation. There was more to it, but now wasn't the time for it.

"She left home how long ago?"

"She was sixteen."

"Maybe it's time for your brother to let it go."

She agreed, but she was too shaken to say so.

His hand moved to her nape, and he kneaded the tense muscles there. "Relax. Everything will work out."

"How? Someone is after my sister. She's on the run for whatever reason—"

"The reason," he explained gently, "is probably the money that was lying on the floor of your room."

"I know." She sighed. "I know she took something from her husband, but I don't believe that's what this is all about. Jarrod has a lot of money. He has a lot of power. Why would he need her or the money and jewels she took from him?"

"A power trip? Maybe he doesn't like to lose his possessions."

"He'll lose a lot more if he gets caught trying to hurt my sister."

"He isn't planning to get caught. Men like him never do. They think they're above the law, too smart to ever be found out." His hand shifted to her shoulder, settled just under her hair.

His touch was light, his hand gentle. He wasn't holding her in place. It would have been easy to walk to the sheriff's car that was pulling up the street. It would have made sense to ask questions about the guy the deputy had taken into custody. She could have done those things, but the cool air felt good on her throbbing cheek, Malone's hand felt good on her shoulder, and she just stood in the shadow of the old trees, trying not to look at the guy the deputy was questioning.

Would he have killed her?

She shuddered, and Malone's hand dropped away. Seconds later, a warm jacket settled around her shoulders. It smelled of smoke and of masculinity, the spicy fresh scent of soap and shampoo and the outdoors.

"Thanks," she murmured, burrowing into it.

"Favor for favor," he responded, and she met his eyes.

"What is that supposed to mean?"

"I give you the jacket, and you tell me why you decided it was smart to leave a safe position and walk into a dangerous one."

For a second, Malone thought Quinn would refuse to answer. She watched him through hooded eyes, the bruise on her cheek dark against her fair skin. He could see it clearly, even with the shadows and the darkness, even with her chin tucked into his coat, he could see that bruise. He wanted to leave her where she was, walk to the guy he'd tackled and repay him the favor.

He'd learned to control his fists and his temper a long time ago. Emotion had no place in situations like this one. It didn't help the victim. It didn't keep a person a step ahead of the bad guys. All it did was cloud a person's thinking and make wise action nearly impossible.

"I was heading to the diner," Quinn finally said. "Everyone in town goes there. It's open all night, and—"

"You were hungry?"

She laughed, the sound hollow and shaky. "No, but I figured my sister had gotten hungry at some point over the past forty-eight hours. The diner is somewhere she could go late at night or early in the morning when fewer people would be around to notice her."

"Good thought," he said, cupping her elbow and leading her out from beneath the trees. He'd seen her getting out of the SUV. He'd watched her walk down the street. He could have stopped her at any time, but he hadn't realized she'd planned to go somewhere. He'd thought she was getting air, and he'd figured she needed space.

Until she'd disappeared from view.

He wouldn't make that mistake again.

"How about next time, you fill me in on the plan before you act on it?" he continued, walking her past the sheriff's cruiser. The perp was in the back of it now, slumped down so far in the seat, Malone couldn't get a good look at his face. It didn't matter. He was in custody. Hopefully, he'd talk.

"I didn't think I was in any danger."

"I didn't think you'd take off and disappear. We were both wrong. Let's not be wrong again. It could end a lot differently than it did tonight."

"Ma'am," one of the deputies called out. "We'd like to take your statement."

It wasn't something Malone wanted to waste time doing—standing around while the sheriff's department asked more questions and realized they had no answers.

Protocol, though.

HEART never interfered with local police efforts. They cooperated fully and they avoided stepping on toes.

And Malone *was* a member of the team.

Despite Chance's words and his response. They butted heads a lot. It was part of what they did, but they never stopped being a team.

"You up for that?" he asked, and Quinn nodded.

"The sooner I get it over with, the sooner I can get to the diner. I have a feeling Tabitha was there. If she was, I know people noticed her."

"She stands out?" If so, that was a good thing. In a town the size of Echo Lake, a stranger would be noticed. A stranger who stood out would be noticed even more.

"She looks rich and polished and very sure of herself. There are plenty of people like that in Echo Lake, but none of them wear it quite so loudly."

"Jewelry?" he asked.

"Understated but very expensive. Same for her clothes. Plus, she's beautiful."

"She's the key to all this, you know," he said as they approached the deputy. "August might be overreacting, but Tabitha's entrance into your life brought everything else into it."

"I know."

"You might be better off taking a vacation, going somewhere and hiding out until your sister is found and the police figure out what's going on. We've got safe houses. HEART can put you up in one until—"

"Would you do that, Malone?" She stopped short and turned to face him. Out from under the shadowy trees, the bruise was even more noticeable, her cheek and jaw swollen. "If it were a member of your family, would you go hide away and let other people solve the problem?"

"No," he answered honestly.

"Then don't ask me to." She started walking again, resolutely heading toward the deputy, the hem of Malone's jacket falling nearly to her knees. He kept forgetting how small she was, but he hadn't forgotten how easily she could be hurt. The guy they'd found in the lake hadn't died of natural causes. The sheriff had brought that piece of news to Quinn's apartment. Blunt-force trauma to the head. That's what the medical examiner had said. Homicide was what the sheriff had said. They'd identified the deceased through fingerprints. The guy was a small-time thug from Las Vegas, Nevada, and his prints had matched the ones found on Tabitha's phone.

Connections everywhere. Tabitha, her husband, Jubilee, a bunch of small-time criminals who seemed intent on getting Tabitha back to her husband.

One of those criminals was dead.

Why?

Had he asked for more money? Found out something he shouldn't have? Had he ceased being useful? Messed up on the assignment?

Maybe the last was closest to the truth. Nothing had been taken from Quinn's apartment. If Malone's theory was correct, Tabitha had waited until her sister left town, and then she'd returned to the apartment, broken in and squatted there, figuring that anyone looking for her would assume she'd left town.

Only the guys who were after her weren't as stupid as she'd thought. They'd tracked her down, nearly taken her in the apartment. Somehow, she'd escaped. Had the murdered man been punished for that?

Too many questions. Until they had answers, Quinn wouldn't be safe.

His cell phone buzzed, and he glanced at it. Boone's number flashed across the screen, and he picked up.

"Malone, here. You in the States yet?"

"You know my schedule. I'm in London. Flight boards in ten minutes. Have you seen her?"

Malone didn't need to ask who he was talking about. "Just briefly."

"And?" Boone asked. He had the information from Chance. Malone knew it, but he repeated what had already been said.

"Red hair. Blue eyes. Tiny."

"Like her mother."

"I never met her mother, but the kid is very small for her age."

"Red hair and blue eyes is a rare combination," Boone said softly. Maybe he was talking to himself, but Malone responded.

"It is, and we've found a connection between her and the cult your wife was in."

"Jarrod Williams, right? Chance sent me the information. It's her, Malone. I'm sure that little girl is my daughter." His voice cracked, the first time Malone had ever heard him sound even close to a breakdown.

"You okay, man?"

"Yeah. I just need a box of doughnuts or something. They don't feed you crumbs on these long flights. I called my wife. She's camping in the CPS lobby waiting with the kids." Boone had married Scout Cramer nearly two years ago after helping her out of some trouble she was in. She'd already had a little girl—a child Boone loved like his own. Now they had a baby together, a little red-haired imp that had the entire family wrapped around her little finger. "She seems to think they'll take pity on her eventually and let her see my…"

"Daughter?"

"It's a hard thing to say after so long, Malone. It's a hard thing to believe that I could actually see her again after all these years. Chance told me her name. Jubilee, right? That's what they've been calling her."

"Yes."

"We won't change it. She's had enough trauma in her life."

"You're a decent guy, Boone," Malone said, and he heard his friend chuckle.

"High praise. You still on your vacation?"

"Finishing up some business first."

"What business?"

Obviously Chance had decided not to fill him in on everything. "We can discuss it after you see your kid."

"If she's mine, Malone. Don't think that's not in the back of my mind. There are a lot of things that have been making this look good, but I've had other times when I thought we might have found her. I'll call you when I land. You can fill me in then."

He disconnected, and Malone shoved the phone in his pocket.

There was nothing he could to do make things

easier for Boone, no action he could take to speed things along. All he could do was work to find some answers that might make sense.

And the first step to that was finding Tabitha.

He hadn't heard from Stella or Chance.

They had to have come up empty.

It was time to do what Quinn had suggested—go to the local diner. It was a hangout for everyone and the perfect place for juicy town gossip.

She was still talking to the deputy, but Malone figured he knew exactly how to speed *that* process along.

NINE

Quinn wanted to sit down.

She didn't know if it was her shaky legs that were making her desperate for a chair or if it was the pulsing pain in the side of her face. Whatever the case, she felt weak, and the more Deputy Leon Ernst assured her that they would throw the book at the guy who'd attacked her, the worse she felt.

She touched the swollen place on the side of her jaw, and Deputy Ernst frowned. "Do you need medical attention? It looks like you've got a lot of bruising there."

"No, but—"

"Yes." Suddenly Malone was beside her, his arm around her waist, his hand splayed against her side. "She does need medical attention."

"I can speak for myself," she sputtered, but neither man seemed to be listening.

"I can call an ambulance. I should have thought to do that before."

"I don't need an ambulance, and I'm not going to the hospital," Quinn said firmly.

"You're pale." Malone ran a finger along her jaw, skimming lightly over the sore spot. "And that's quite a bruise. Maybe you just need to sit down, put some ice on it. Maybe have some juice or a coffee. Know anywhere where that might be able to happen?"

My place, she almost said, but that didn't seem to be the answer he was going for, and her sluggish brain wasn't able to conjure anything different.

"Like," Malone nudged, "a coffee shop? A diner?"

There! That was it! The diner.

"Yes. Another three blocks down. Betty Sue's place."

"You could just sit in my cruiser," Deputy Ernst offered. "I'd be happy to find some ice for your bruise."

"She's probably hungry, too," Malone suggested, and the deputy frowned.

"I'm getting the impression that you don't think she should be interviewed any longer."

"Only because I have the impression that the perpetrator is already in custody. Can you take Quinn's statement later?"

"I already got it. I was just clarifying a few things. Which I guess I could do tomorrow morning. Do you want to come to the station then, Ms. Robertson?"

Not really, but it was better than hashing it out on the street corner. "Sure. I can do that."

"I'll be in the office until ten. If you need to meet later than that, give me a call." He pressed a business card into her palm.

"Thank you."

"Don't mention it, ma'am." He gave a quick nod and headed toward his cruiser.

Which meant she and Malone were free to go.

The problem was, her legs didn't seem to want to work. No matter how many times she told them to move forward, they stayed stuck in place.

"Maybe you really do need an ambulance," Malone said, cupping her face, his dark gaze tracing the curve of her cheek, stopping for just a moment on her jaw. "He really did get a couple of good hits in. I should have been there sooner."

"I'm the one who decided to go off on my own."

"If I'd been paying more attention to you, you wouldn't have," he growled.

"Are you saying that somehow you could have stopped me?" she demanded, her legs suddenly unstuck, her body finally moving forward. "Because, I can tell you right now, I would have gone anyway. As a matter of fact…"

He was smiling, a mischievous smile that reminded her of the way one of her students looked when they got one over on her.

"You did that on purpose, didn't you?" she accused, and his smile broadened.

"What?"

"Got my mind off the apartment and the blood and—"

"Tabitha missing? You needed your mind off it. At least for a few minutes."

"I just don't understand it." She led him to the end of the block, turned the corner onto 5th. She could see the lights from the diner up ahead, and could imagine hot coffee sliding down her throat, warm pie filling her stomach.

"Understand what?"

"Tabitha was in the church or near it. I heard her calling for me." At least, she'd thought it was her sister. "Why did she run off when help arrived?"

"Maybe she didn't see the help. Maybe she just saw the guy who attacked you. In which case, the better question would be—why didn't she run to help?"

"That sounds like something August would say," she accused, but he didn't seem bothered by the comparison.

"Your brother might have an issue with your sister, but he wouldn't be wrong. What kind of person sees her sister or brother in trouble and doesn't run to the rescue?"

"Someone who is scared?"

"I hope," he said very quietly and very clearly, "that I am never too afraid to help someone who needs it."

He pushed open the diner door, motioned for her to walk.

She wanted to tell him that he had no idea what it was like to be vulnerable, that it was easy to judge someone when you'd never even spent a minute in that person's shoes. She turned to face him as he entered the diner behind her, saw the scar on his face, the thick line of it marring his skin, and she thought that maybe he did know. That maybe he'd sacrificed a lot for people he cared about.

"What happened?" she asked, the question just there without her even thinking she was going to speak it.

He must have known what she was referring to.

His fingers skimmed across the scar. "My battalion and I were under attack in Iraq after our Humvee was disabled by an IED. A few of us managed to get out of the vehicle and fight hand to hand. I was the only one who survived."

"I'm so sorry, Malone." She touched his hand, and he turned his palm so that they could link fingers. Palm to palm, she could see the dry warmth of his skin, the roughness of the calluses. She ran her thumb across his scarred knuckles, imagined him fighting to stay alive, too keep his comrades alive.

"Don't cry," he said. "It happened a long time ago."

"I'm not," she lied, because she could feel the tears burning behind her eyes and knew if she let them they really would start falling. "And a long time doesn't take away the sting of loss."

"You'd know that as well as me." He didn't release her hand as Holly Andrews ran over, her waitressing uniform as wrinkled as her face.

"While I live and breathe! If it isn't my old friend Quinn." She smiled broadly, patted her overly processed hair. "And who is this adorable young man you've brought with you?"

She patted Malone's arm, and he gave her a look that would have made other women run. Not Holly. She liked men—old, young, ugly, handsome—she didn't care, she flirted with them. And, of course, Malone wasn't old or ugly. He was handsome, fit, charming.

"Malone is…a friend of mine," Quinn said, and Holly smirked.

"Ah. I see. Mitts off, huh?"

"No. Yes. What I mean," she tried, more flustered than she had any reason to be, "is that—"

"We're here together and we'd like a seat." Malone squeezed her hand, and that's when she realized they were still standing like they had been—palm to palm, fingers linked.

"Sure, hon," Holly said without ire. She might like men, but she also liked gossip. *Quinn and some good-looking guy with a scar. Swoon!* Quinn could almost hear the words. Holly probably wouldn't even wait five seconds after they left to say them to someone.

"You're frowning," Malone said as she dropped into a booth, the vinyl seat squeaking as she moved close to the window.

"Am I?" She grabbed a menu even though she didn't need one and opened it up so that she wouldn't have to look in Malone's face. He had an uncanny ability to read her, and she didn't want him to know just how uncomfortable with this she was.

This?

Coffee with some guy who was helping her out?

There was nothing wrong with that, no reason to feel uneasy about it, but she felt like there was. As if somewhere, Cory might be watching, his heart aching because she was with someone else.

"Stupid," she muttered, and Malone cocked

his head to the side, his dark eyes spearing straight into hers.

"I'm assuming you're not talking about me, so…who's stupid?"

"No one."

"And yet you said it, so how about I order coffee and pie, and you tell me what's going on?" He motioned Holly over, asked her to bring coffee and two slices of hot apple pie. One with ice cream. One without.

She loved apple pie.

She also loved ice cream.

And, she'd forgotten how much she loved sitting across the table from a man, watching his hands smooth over the tabletop or tap a rhythm on the windowsill.

She looked away, trying to focus on the darkness outside, the quiet, charming street with its pretty shops and lights, but she could see Malone reflected in the glass, the scar a vivid reminder of what he'd survived.

He didn't speak. Not as the coffee arrived. Not as the pie was served. The plain pie for Malone. The one with ice cream for Quinn. He didn't speak as he poured cream into her cup, opened a packet of sugar and poured it on top.

"Maybe I don't like either of those," she muttered through the lump in her throat.

"Don't you?"

"Yes." She finally turned to face him, caught her breath at the look in his eyes—compassion, empathy, concern and something else, a hint of what she was feeling, what she wanted to deny...attraction.

"Then, why complain?"

"Because I didn't tell you I liked those things. Or that I wanted apple pie with ice cream."

"If you want something else—"

"Whether I want this or not, isn't the point."

"Then what is, Quinn? Because the way I see it, we came in here to ask about your sister and to get some sugar in you. I'm not thinking that's anything to get worked up about."

"How did you know?" She stabbed a bite of pie, shoveled it into her mouth, her throat still so tight she wasn't sure she could swallow it.

"About the pie? Your brother mentioned it to me when I got to his house. He'd just pulled an apple pie out of the freezer. Said he liked to make sure he had apple pie and ice cream every time you came, so he always kept one in the freezer. Your mom used to make it for your birthday."

"That's right." Now the lump was even bigger, because not only was she struggling with attraction to someone who wasn't Cory, she was making a fool of herself over it.

"Same for the cream and sugar. He had bucket

load of both, because you don't like coffee without it."

"Also true."

"What did you think?" he asked, taking a sip of coffee. His was black, and that didn't surprise her. He seemed like the kind of guy who'd have coffee without cream, pie without ice cream, relationships without complications. He also seemed like the kind of guy who'd be in it 100 percent, no holding back, no keeping a little of himself away. Whatever *it* was—work, family, love.

"Did you think I had mind-reading abilities?" he prodded, a half smile softening his face. He looked younger sitting there with a cup of coffee in his hand and a plate of pie on the table in front of him.

"You have a lot of skills, Malone. Anything is possible."

He laughed at that, outright and loud enough for Millie Winslow to look up from her nightly bowl of mulligan stew. Most people in town wouldn't touch the stuff, but Betty Sue, the diner's owner, made it anyway, giving it out free to anyone who was hungry.

Millie was never hungry.

She had a huge house with a huge kitchen and a huge pantry. She also had plenty of money, thanks to her ex-husband. She was frugal to a fault, though, and never paid for anything she could get for free.

"Can you be quiet?" she snapped. "Some of us like to enjoy our meals in peace."

"Some of us," Holly muttered as she refilled Malone's coffee, "need to enjoy our evenings without having to see the Scrooge every time we turn our heads."

"Did you say something, dear?" Millie asked, wiping her mouth with a cloth napkin she'd probably brought from home.

"Nothing you need to hear."

"Like I didn't hear you tell that woman that she could probably get work shining my truck-load of silver? She could have broken into my house, you know. A stranger with a *tattoo*! Of all the people to tell my business to."

A tattoo?

Tabitha had more than one. Most had been covered by the clothes she'd been wearing when she'd dropped Jubilee off, but there was one on her wrist that might have been visible.

"Was there a stranger here recently?" Quinn asked, trying to keep her tone casual. If Holly got an inkling of how eager she was to hear the answer, she might clam up. At least for a while. She liked to be convinced to share gossip, made to feel as if the truth had to be yanked out of her.

"There was!" Millie huffed, standing up and leaving her half-full bowl of soup on the table. "One of those beautiful kinds. You know the ones I mean. They sneak around behind a woman's back and steal her man."

"She seemed nice enough to me," Holly said with a shrug. "And I've got a sixth sense for man stealing, backstabbing females."

"Did she say where she was from?" Malone asked, finally scooping up a bite of his pie.

"You guys looking for her?" Holly asked, her drawn-on eyebrows raising a quarter of an inch.

"I'm looking for my sister. She stopped by my house a couple of nights ago, and I haven't seen her since." Honesty was always the best policy, so Quinn gave it a shot. "Her name is Tabitha Williams. She's a beautiful woman. Blond hair. Perfect skin."

"A rock the size of a grape on her hand," Holly added. "She's the lady who was in here. Said her name was Lacey."

"That's her middle name."

"She hiding from someone? She had bruises on her neck." Holly's gaze dropped to Quinn's jaw, and she scowled. "What happened, doll? I was so busy looking at your man, I didn't notice that you took a hit. He do it to you?" She jabbed a thumb in Malone's direction. "If he did, I can find ways to make him pay."

"No!" Quinn protested. "And he's not my man."

"He should be. The guy is hot. You're hot," she repeated, smiling at Malone. "Too young for me, though. As for Lacey. She was looking for work."

"And bigmouth told her all about my fancy silver. She'll probably break into my house—"

"Enough," Malone said so quietly, Quinn barely heard.

Despite the distance between them, Millie must have. Her mouth gapped open, then slammed shut. "You have no right—"

"You have no right speculating about someone that has done nothing to you. If the woman shows up at your house begging for silver or asking for money, file a police report. Otherwise, let it go."

"I have every right to protect what's mine."

"Maybe you should go home and do that then," Holly suggested, and Millie stomped away, leaving her cloth napkin at the table.

"She'll be back for that," Holly said. "That woman is tighter than a size-six ring on a size-seven finger. Now, who punched you, Quinn? I'm going to take him out."

"The sheriff has him in custody."

"Good. I've been feeling a little jittery since they found that body in the lake." She shuddered. "Guy was in here the same night as your sister."

The words were like ice water in the face. "You're sure?"

"As sure as I am that you're sitting in that booth. He came in about twenty minutes after your sister, ordered coffee and a sandwich to go. Said he was from out of town. Just passing through. That's the way he said it."

"Did he give you his name?"

"No, and the sheriff didn't tell me squat, either. I called his office to see if it really was the same guy, and no one called me back. Story was front page of the newspaper this morning, though. They said the guy was wearing black dress pants, a button up shirt and a blue jacket. Now, let me ask you something. You ever seen a homeless person dressed like that?"

"Yes," Malone answered, and Holly scowled.

"Not around here you haven't. That's what the guy was wearing when he came into the diner. It's what the dead guy was wearing. Coincidence? I don't think so."

"Did he tell you where he was traveling from? Where he was heading to?" Malone asked, and Holly shook her head.

"Nah. He was pretty tight-lipped. I'm thinking he was involved in some kind of organized crime ring, you know? Those kinds of people get dumped in lakes all the time."

"They also like quiet places to meet. Did he ask you anything about the area?" Malone took a bite of pie, then scooped up a spoonful of her melting ice cream.

Quinn thought he planned to eat it, but he nudged it up to her lips instead. "Eat."

"I'm—" He shoved the ice cream in her mouth and smiled.

Holly laughed. "Girl! You've got yourself a winner there. As for that guy who died…he didn't ask." She frowned. "Actually, now that you mention it, he did ask a few questions that seemed odd."

"Like?" Malone ate another bite of pie, but his attention was on Holly, his gaze completely focused.

"He asked where the local elementary school was. Said he had a daughter who'd be attending kindergarten next year. He was wondering what the schools were like here."

Kindergarten?

Had that been the truth? A random choice? Or had he been looking for the school because he'd wanted to find Quinn?

She met Malone's eyes. He looked as intrigued as she felt.

"Anything else?" he asked.

"Yeah. He said he'd like to do a little boating and fishing. Asked if there were any marinas around where he could rent a boat. I told him about Tom Wilken's place."

"I wonder if he ever made it there," Quinn said more to herself than to Malone and Holly. There was no way either of them could know the answer.

"He did," Holly piped up so confidently, Quinn had to believe she was telling the truth. Or thought she was.

"Did you hear that from someone?" Malone finished off his pie, pushed the plate into the middle of the table and grabbed his coffee cup.

"Tom Wilkens was in with the pastor this morning. They both had the special. Two eggs. Sausage. Hash browns. Not that it matters. I just tend to keep track of customer orders. Anyway, I overheard Tom telling the pastor that one of his flat bottom boats was missing. Had it last night. Didn't have it when he got in to work."

"Did Tom think the dead man took his boat?" It's what Quinn would have thought, but thinking something didn't make it true.

"I have no idea, but it makes sense doesn't it? Some outsider comes to town, goes to the marina and steals a boat with his buddy. The buddy gets mad, and the next thing you know, there's a body in the water."

Or, some guy comes to town, steals a boat thinking he can use it to dispose of a body and then...

What?

He calls someone? Asks for some backup? Gets himself in trouble with the boss?

"Do you think you can put this in a to-go container?" Malone asked, lifting the plate of pie Quinn hadn't finished.

"Sure." Holly hurried away, a bounce in her steps, a sway in her hips. She was excited by the things that had been happening in town.

Quinn was not.

She was scared and tired and wishing that she could have had just a second to talk to her sister, make sure that she was doing okay, ask her what in the world she'd gotten herself into.

Gotten Quinn into.

At least Tabitha had made sure Jubilee was safe.

The police and FBI could say what they wanted, they could think what they wanted, but there was love between those two. Love could make people do stupid things, and Quinn preferred to think that was what had motivated Tabitha. Not the greed that might have enticed her to steal money and jewelry, not some un-

founded or well-founded anger at her husband—
love for the child she'd mothered for at least two
and a half years.

Then I met Jubilee, and I was hooked.

Jubilee was the motivation.

She was the key to everything that had happened.

Quinn believed that.

Now she just had to find a way to prove it.

TEN

Quinn didn't say much as Malone paid for the pie and the coffee and led her outside. That surprised and worried him. She wasn't a quiet person. She said what she thought, she went after what she needed. So, why was she walking beside him, head down, gaze on the ground, not a word on her lips?

Fatigue?

Fear?

Probably a little of both, but there was more to it than that, and he wanted to know what.

"Penny for your thoughts," he said, the words drifting on still night air.

"They're only worth a penny?" she responded, looking up from the ground and meeting his eyes. She'd never gotten ice for the bruise, and it was a gray-black smudge across her jaw and the side of her face.

"And pie. And a cup of coffee." He handed her the carryout coffee cup. He'd added extra sugar to it before they'd left, and she grimaced as she took a sip.

"You mean a cup of sugar," she said, her pace brisk.

"You need the calories and the quick energy."

"I need to find my sister, and I need to know the truth about Jubilee. She's the key, Malone. I know she is."

"How?" Because, the way he was seeing things, the little girl was a pawn in a game that had turned deadly serious. Same for Quinn. Both were a means to an end. The end being Jarrod getting his wife back for whatever reason was driving him—jealousy, rage, revenge.

"Maybe Jarrod is worried about going to jail for claiming her as his child when she wasn't? I think you've found evidence that proves he was the one that took her out of the cult. Maybe he's trying to get her back so that no one will know what he did."

"You're forgetting that the FBI has already called him. They've had open lines of communication about Jubilee. Sure, his story can be proved to be a lie, but he can claim he got scared, tried to cover up because he's an innocent man and never been in trouble with the law before."

"Innocent men don't put tracking devices in their kid's booster seat."

"They do if they have more money than sense and they don't trust their spouses." He'd seen it more than once in his line of work.

"My sister is a lot of things, Malone. I know that. But she loved Jubilee. I could see it in the way she talked to her, and Jubilee loved her. They might not be genetically related, but their bond is strong."

"Meaning?"

"Something happened. Tabitha and Jubilee were both bruised when they arrived at my place. Tabitha isn't the kind of person who'd let someone hit her and not walk out. At least, I don't think she is, and I definitely don't believe she'd let a child be hurt."

"What do you think happened?" She was on the track of something. Malone could sense it. While everyone else had been focusing on Tabitha's past, her criminal record, the items she'd taken from her husband, Quinn had been looking for the truth.

"That something scared Tabitha so much, she knew she had to run and take Jubilee with her. Not just the abuse. My sister would have taken pictures and gone to the police and taken Jarrod for everything he had if that's all there was to it."

"She could have gone to the police anyway."

"She told me that Jarrod had a lot of connections. She begged me not to contact law enforcement until after Jubilee had been brought to her biological father."

"Because she didn't want to be caught with her hands full of stolen property?" he suggested, and she shook her head.

"That's what everyone believes. It's what Jarrod wants everyone to believe, but I think she wanted time."

"To do what?"

"Prove whatever it is she suspects? Hide before she lets the police know what her husband had done? It could be anything. Until we talk to her, we won't know the truth."

"She's not making that easy."

"Would you, if you thought someone wanted you dead?"

He wouldn't, but he had plenty of friends and family who'd come to his rescue if he needed it, who'd keep him hidden, work behind the scenes to prove his innocence or to keep him safe. He'd *had* plenty of people come to his rescue over the years. Someone like Tabitha wouldn't have known where to run, whom to ask for help. She'd lived her life on a surface level, and that never created good connections.

"You said that you and your sister hadn't seen each other in years?"

"We hadn't. She came to my wedding, got

drunk as a skunk and had to be escorted off the premises."

"I wonder why she flew all the way to Maine instead of flying to Maryland and asking August for help." It would have made more sense, would have been the safer option.

"You've seen how August feels about her. He'd have called the police immediately."

"That might have been the better option. Look at the mess she's in. The mess she's gotten *you* in."

"It would have been her story against Jarrod's, and she'd have been standing there with her pockets and hands full of stolen property, claiming that he was the bad guy. Eventually, the police might have checked out her claims that Jubilee wasn't Jarrod's child, but what if he'd left the country before then? What if he'd harmed Jubilee, or hidden her away? Let's cut through here." She took his hand, her hand cold in his as she tugged him to a path that seemed to meander through thick trees. "It'll be a lot quicker."

"Quicker than what?"

"Walking through town to get to the marina. I want to talk to Tom."

"It's late. Are you sure he'll be there?"

"His house is a block away. Really pretty

view of the lake. I went there for lunch one Sunday after church."

"A short cut through the woods when there's a murderer walking around might not be the best idea, Quinn." He stopped.

Cold air swirled around them, a hint of winter and moisture in it. They couldn't be far from the lake. He could see lights through the trees, a glint of water, but someone had been murdered the previous night, and Malone wasn't into taking needless chances.

"It's a quarter mile through the trees. A mile and a half if we have to go around them."

"I like shortcuts. When I know what I'm going to run into on them. I'll call Chance and have him meet us here. We'll go to the Marina together."

"I thought he was out looking for Tabitha. That's a better use of his time."

"A better use of his time—the only use of it that matters to me right now—is keeping you safe. Have you forgotten that you were attacked less than an hour ago?"

"No, but—"

"This is what we do, Quinn," he said, cutting her off. "Don't tie our hands and expect that we can protect you."

"I didn't ask you for protection," she mumbled, tugging her hand out of his. "I didn't ask you for anything. All I wanted was to get Jubilee back where she belonged. The rest of this is a nightmare, and I just want it to be over."

She was close to her breaking point, and if he wasn't careful he was going to push her right over the edge.

It wasn't what he wanted.

He needed her strong, and he needed her focused.

He also needed her to cooperate.

"Listen to me," he said, his hands resting on her biceps, his fingers curved lightly around slim, firm muscles. "You and I have exactly the same goals. We've got to work together on this, and we've got to be smart about it." His hands slid to her shoulders, his thumbs brushing silky skin. "You're running on emotion, and I'm running on logic. If you think about it, you'll realize that I'm right—putting ourselves in danger isn't going to keep Tabitha safe."

She frowned, but didn't pull away from his hold.

"I really wish I could argue with that. But I can't, so call your boss and tell him we need a ride."

"That's the spirit," he said, reaching for his cell phone. He hadn't heard from Chance or Stella. They must still be on the hunt for

Tabitha. He texted his location and hit send, took Quinn's arm and led her to the curb.

"Let's wait here," he said, pulling her down so they were both sitting at the edge of the sidewalk.

"Waiting seems like a huge waste of time." She pulled a blade of grass from a crack in the sidewalk and ripped it apart. "And I know you agree, because you definitely don't seem like the kind of person who likes to sit idle."

"You're right, but this isn't sitting idle. This is waiting for a ride that can take us where we want to go." And, he hoped it arrived soon, because he was getting that feeling again—the one that said things weren't quite what they seemed, that maybe danger wasn't as far away as he was hoping.

"What's your family like, Malone?" Quinn asked, pulling up another blade of grass. "Because I'm hoping it's just as crazy as mine."

He smiled, thinking about the siblings and cousins he'd helped raise, all the trouble that they'd gotten into and that Malone and his grandfather had helped them out of. "They are."

"Do you have a big family?"

"Eleven kids all living in an old farmhouse with one bathroom and three bedrooms."

"Wow, your parents had their hands full."

"My grandparents, actually. My parents and

aunt and uncle were killed by a drunk driver when I was eleven. After that, Granddad and Grandmom raised me, my four siblings and my six cousins on their farm. I was the oldest, so I helped out with the younger kids a lot, and I can assure you that every single one of them was nuts."

"That must have been tough."

"Losing my parents was. Living with my grandparents…it was good. It taught me a lot about the value of family. It taught me everything I know about love and faith and keeping on. You learned that, too, Quinn. That's why you're fighting so hard for a sister you haven't seen in years. It's why your brother keeps an apple pie in his freezer. It's why Tabitha made sure Jubilee was safe before she did anything else. In the midst of whatever craziness your family had, the three of you were taught what to value."

"I guess you're right."

"No guessing. Love is the thread that's sewn you three together. That thread is made of steel, and it can't be broken."

"Death can break it," she said, the fear in her voice palpable.

"Even death can't break love's hold. Look at you," he said, lifting her right hand and touching the narrow gold band. "You haven't stopped loving your husband."

"No, but it's not the same."

"Would you want it to be? Would you want to still have that great love for him, still be tied to him even though he's no longer tied to you?" he asked, even though it was none of his business. Even though he shouldn't care.

He *did* care.

He wasn't so much of a coward that he couldn't admit it.

He'd never wanted to get in a deep relationship with anyone. He'd never wanted marriage, family, the kinds of things his parents and grandparents had cherished. He'd done his time, helped raise a bunch of kids before entering the military. That had always seemed like enough. Until recently. Until his busy schedule had become just one job after another, until he'd realized that his nieces and nephews were growing up and didn't even really know him.

Until he'd looked around and saw friends getting married, having kids, settling into family, and he'd still been chasing after the next adrenaline high.

Looking at Quinn, her shoulders hunched as she stared across the street, that ring glinting in the moonlight, he thought he'd been a fool to think that there would never come a time when he'd want more than what he had.

"Quinn." He lifted her hand again, heard her sigh. "*Would* you want it to be?"

She turned her head slowly, and he could see the tears in her eyes, knew that she understood what he was asking—was there room for someone else? Was she able to let go of what she'd had so that she could grasp something new?

"It feels like betraying him," she said. Not an answer to the question, but he thought it was all she could give.

"When it doesn't—" he stood, pulled her to her feet "—let me know, okay?"

She nodded as a car turned onto the road, sped toward them without any indication that it planned to slow. Not Stella and Chance. That was for sure.

Malone yanked Quinn toward the trees, shoving her behind a wide-trunked oak.

"Get down," he yelled, pulling his firearm as the vehicle jumped the curb.

Tires squealed, brakes screamed, gunfire exploded through the trees. Quinn wanted to run, but she couldn't leave Malone behind. She scurried through dead leaves and pine needles, crawling on her hands and knees, her heart pounding frantically. She needed to find a weapon, some way to help if Malone got into trouble.

Her palm scraped over tree roots, and she dug through the leaves, hoping to find a stick or a rock. The world had gone silent and graveyard still. Not an animal or bird moving through the trees.

She wanted to call for Malone, make sure he wasn't lying injured somewhere, but she knew if she did it might be both of their death sentences.

You're running on emotion. I'm running on logic.

He'd been right about that.

She couldn't afford to mess this up. She needed to be careful, methodical. She ran her hands through the dead leaves, finally felt the thick end of a fallen branch. She pulled it out as she stood, trying to be as silent as possible. Still no movement in the woods, no doors slamming or footsteps pounding. Headlights illuminated the path she'd planned to take, and she stayed out of their range, ducking into the shadowy fold of the dense undergrowth, creeping back toward the road. She'd circle around, see if she could get a better look at the vehicle and whoever was in it. See if she could find Malone.

Would you want it to be the same?

His words echoed through her head, mixing with the uneven thump of her heart as she moved closer to the road. She'd been too much of a coward to say she wouldn't, too much of a fool to admit that she felt herself moving on, letting go.

Maybe she just hadn't wanted to admit it to herself.

Maybe she was too afraid to be hurt again, to fall in love and say goodbye again.

Somewhere to her right, a twig snapped, the sound chilling her blood.

She froze, her hand sweaty around the jagged edges of the stick, her heart thumping rapidly.

Leaves crackled under someone's feet.

Not Malone. He moved through woods as silently as a cat.

She pressed back against an old pine tree, the prickly bark digging through her clothes. A dove called from somewhere deep in the woods. Another one answered.

It took a moment for her to realize it was a signal.

Malone and his team, or someone else?

She tightened her grip on the stick, the silence of the forest enveloping her again. If she looked carefully, she could see the lake through the woods, the water glinting with reflected moonlight.

The dove called again. This time closer. Seconds later, the headlights of the car went out, and the world plunged into darkness.

ELEVEN

She needed to move.

She could not keep standing in the shelter of the tree, hoping for the best. She had to find Malone or find help.

Quinn eased around the tree trunk, tried to see into the blackness. Nothing moved. No more dove calls or snapping twigs. She could have been alone in the woods, but she knew she wasn't. People were there, and if she wasn't careful, she'd run into one of them.

She tightened her grip on the stick, took a step away from the tree. Someone grabbed her, throwing a hand over her mouth so quickly she didn't have time to scream.

"Shhhh!" The voice wasn't Malone, and she panicked, kicking backward, connecting with a shin.

Her assailant didn't release his hold, just leaned down and whispered. "It's Chance. And I bruise easy, so lay off."

"Malone," she mumbled against his hand.

"He's chasing after the guy who was in the car."

"What—?"

"How about we talk about it once you're safe?"

"I'm not worried about being safe, I'm worried about Malone!" she protested as he hurried her to the road, waved at someone she couldn't see.

Headlights flooded the street, and the SUV pulled up beside them. Chance hurried Quinn into the backseat, slammed the door and slapped the roof. Then he was gone, running back the way he'd come.

The SUV rolled forward, turned onto Lake Way, a GPS device spouting out directions as Stella drove, her expression grim and tight.

"You're a lot of trouble, you know that?" she said.

"I'm not trying to be."

"Apparently you don't have to try. It just happens when you're around. Bet that sister of yours is the same way."

"Did you find her?" Quinn shifted, trying to see out the back window. Where was Malone? Chance had said he was okay, but would he stay okay? She'd heard gunfire. Had Malone been the one shooting, or had the bullets been flying toward him?

She tried not to think about him, lying bleeding and wounded, but she couldn't stop the image from filling her head.

"No sign of your sister. She's as wily as you are. But we've got an idea where she was heading. There's an old factory just outside of town. Abandoned. You know the one I'm talking about?"

"Factory?" She tried to think of the building Stella was talking about.

"Factory. Shop. I don't know what it is. A couple of stories high. Boarded-up windows?"

"The tannery?" The place had been in its heyday a hundred years ago, when there was a premium for leather goods and hunting hadn't been regulated. It had closed in the sixties, when the old-fashioned process of tanning hides had been too expensive and time-consuming to be lucrative.

"Quinn, you're the one who lives in this town. I'm just passing through on my way back to a normal life," she said wearily.

"It's on the north side of town, right?"

"Yes."

"That's the tannery. It's been closed for decades."

"Which makes it a good place for people to

squat. We talked to some locals. They seemed to think that if someone wanted to hide, that'd be the place to do it."

"Did you tell the sheriff what you suspect?"

"We did one better than that. We went ourselves. Didn't have time to get in, thanks to Malone's SOS, but one of the boards on a back window had been taken down. Seemed like an easy access point. Once we get this newest mess cleared up, we're heading back."

"Shouldn't the sheriff be told about this newest mess?" If Quinn had her phone, she'd have already called, but she had no way to contact anyone. Not the sheriff. Not her brother.

Not Malone, and he was the one she most wanted to hear from.

"Trust me, that grumpy old man has been informed. Your brother has been at the station for hours, trying to get information about Tabitha. I texted him and told him to send the old guy this way."

"Sheriff Lock isn't old or grumpy."

"He acts old, and he was sure grumpy with me when I spoke with him earlier. Guess the guy isn't used to dealing with chaos."

"Echo Lake is usually calm and quiet." Quinn had loved it from the moment she'd visited for the first time, met all Cory's friends, his family, the people he'd grown up with and loved.

Now that he was gone, she was part of that network, as completely enmeshed in it as he had once been.

"It seems like it. It's pretty, too. Trees and water and beautiful old houses. I bet there's a bed-and-breakfast somewhere, right? Some huge old Victorian that some old lady inherited from her family."

"Blue Bonnet Hill. It's on a double lot in the middle of town."

"I knew it!" Stella said. "I've always wanted to live in a place like this. When my husband was alive, we used to…"

"What?"

"Nothing. Just silly kid stuff dreaming about things that are never going to happen."

"Like moving to a little town and raising a family?" Quinn guessed.

"Like I said, it was silly kid's stuff. Sometimes it works out for people." She pulled into Tom's Marina, and shifted so she could meet Quinn's eyes. "When it does, it's pretty special. Look at my friend Boone. He's married now, with two beautiful kids, and soon he's going to be reunited with the child he's spent five years searching for. Everything he's hoped for is working out."

"What about you, Stella? What are you hoping will work out?"

"Us finding your sister and me getting back home. When you get to be my age, it takes a little more rest to look good, and I wouldn't want to look rough for my date." She patted her unlined cheeks and smiled, but there was a hint of sadness in her eyes.

"Your age? What are you? Twenty-seven?"

"Add a few years to that and then multiply it for all the stress in my life. Come on. Let's go find the guy you and Malone were planning to talk to." She opened the door, her gaze scanning the empty parking lot. She didn't seem nervous, but Quinn didn't suppose she had any reason to be. She'd probably been in a lot worse circumstances than these, facing a lot more daunting odds.

"What about the men?" Quinn asked as she got out of the SUV.

"If they get into trouble, they'll let me know, and I'll call in the cavalry. Otherwise, our assignment is this." With that, she grabbed the hem of Quinn's shirt and tugged her into motion.

The guy was there.

Malone could hear him moving through the trees somewhere ahead. Behind him, sirens blared as the sheriff and his deputies arrived. They could take a look at the car, figure out where it had come from. They could help with the search, find the perp, bring him in for questioning, but they wouldn't be able to stop what had been set in motion. The only one who could do that was Tabitha.

She held the key to this.

She knew what she'd heard or seen or experienced. She understood the power she had over Jarrod's future. And it had to be a lot of power because a guy like Jarrod Williams didn't scare easily, and he was scared. No one sent this much manpower if there wasn't a lot at stake.

Money?

Business?

Freedom?

All of the above?

Malone slipped through dense foliage, moving toward the area he thought the perp had gone. The guy they'd caught in Pennsylvania had said he and two other men had been hired to find Jubilee. They'd taken two into custody. If they assumed that the dead man was the third, it stood to reason this fourth guy was Charles Libby. If they got their hands on him, they might get confirmation that *the boss* was Jarrod Williams.

He motioned for Chance to flank to the right, try to get in front of the perp before he made it to the lake. Malone could see it through the trees, hear the water lapping against the shore line. The woods must front to a small beach. If Malone were on the run from the police, then that would be the last place he'd want to be. Too open.

But it was the direction the perp seemed to be heading.

Could there be a dock? A boat?

Maybe the boat that had been stolen from the marina?

He moved cautiously, gun still in his hand, body humming with adrenaline. His senses were most alive when he was on the hunt, moving into dangerous territory to find or free the lost, but he was finding that he couldn't live in this place, that his mind was starting to crave normalcy, that every time he visited Tennessee, he thought of how nice it would be to have a place like that to return to, some*one* to return to.

Quiet evenings spent talking.

Fireside chats on winter mornings.

A couple of kids running around.

Maybe a dog.

Big dreams for a guy who'd never wanted any of those things. Maybe that was part of the process of maturing or maybe it came from seeing the worst parts of life—the hard things, the sorrow, the tragedies. That made a guy yearn for a little normalcy, it made him crave the innocuous everyday troubles that most people complained about—broken water heaters, flat tires, kids throwing fits. Those were the easy things when a person really knew what the hard things were.

And Malone did.

Something splashed into the water, the sound a jarring note in the eerie silence. Another splash, and Malone sprinted forward, clearing the trees and racing out onto the beach. Two hundred yards away, a dock stretched out into the water, a pretty little houseboat tied up beside it, blocking his view of what lay beyond. There were no lights on in the boat, no sign that anyone lived there.

He raced toward the dock, Chance running up beside him, the sound of oars slapping against the water spurring them both on.

"Hold on!" Chance pulled him back when they reached the dock. "You said he was armed, and we have no idea where he is. Until we've got a clear view of the area, we need to take it slow."

"He fired three rounds. He might be out of ammunition, because he hasn't fired since."

"Either that, or he realized he was wasting ammunition and was holding off until he had a clearer shot. Let's play this safe. I don't want to lose a team member."

"I'm off the team, remember?" Malone stepped onto the deck, staying close to the houseboat as he moved.

"You've been reinstated. As much as it pains me to admit it, you're an asset to HEART."

"You must be tired, Chance, if you're talking like that."

"Just want to make sure that you know you're appreciated. Some people on the team say that I'm not generous enough with the praise."

"Some people meaning Stella?"

"*Some people*. Meaning people."

"Well, unlike those people, I'm not all that concerned with being praised." He stopped at the end of the house boat. The dock stretched out another twenty feet, moonlight glittering on the water beyond it. He couldn't see the perp; and the lapping of waves against pilings masked any other noise that he might have heard. "He's out of view. I'm going to have to go out in the open."

"Cautiously," Chance muttered, following Malone out of the shadow of the boat.

The guy was a few hundred yards out, rowing hard for the far shore. Malone could see him clearly. Dark hair. Middle-aged.

"May as well come back now," he called. "The police will be waiting when you reach the other side."

No response.

Not that Malone expected one.

He could have jumped into the lake and gone after the guy, but he could hear sirens screaming in the distance, could see them flashing in the trees on the other side of the lake. Sheriff Lock knew what he was doing. He had men on the ground, and unless Malone missed his guess, there'd be a state helicopter with a search light appearing soon. He could already hear the thump of helicopter rotors in the distance.

"Looks like he's not any better at listening than you are," Chance muttered.

"Looks like it isn't going to matter. He'll be in custody in minutes."

"And we'll be answering more questions asked by the local PD. This is why I like to keep out of trouble when we're in the States. It wastes time. Time I don't have."

"You have somewhere more important to be?"

"Yeah. In DC making sure Boone and his family are doing okay. This stuff—" he gestured to the lake, the cruiser that had just appeared on the opposite shore, the helicopter that was a dot on the horizon "—is just incidental. It's not what HEART is about. What our company is about is what happens after the chaos and the trouble and the gunfights—people finally being in each other's arms again. Looks like the perp is changing directions, hoping to find a safer place to land. Let's go deal with the questions, so we can both move on."

He turned away from the boat and walked off the dock.

Malone stood where he was, watching the perp turn circles as he struggled to figure out a way to escape. Malone could have told him it was useless, but he didn't waste his breath. As Chance had said, they had more important places to be.

TWELVE

They'd come up empty.

No information on the missing boat except that it was still missing. None of Tom's neighbors had noticed anyone or anything out of the ordinary. No phone call from Chance or Malone, either. At least that's what Stella had said when they'd gotten back in the SUV. Quinn looked at the dashboard clock. Only five minutes ago.

"Do you think—?"

"They aren't dead."

"You haven't heard from either of them," she pointed out.

"I'd have heard if something happened."

"What if they can't contact you?"

"They can. We have a system set up."

"What kind of system?"

"The kind that always seems to get me stuck with people who ask a lot of questions," she grumbled, pulling up in front of Quinn's apartment. Crime-scene tape stretched across the bottom of the staircase. More blocked the front door.

"I guess they don't want us here," Quinn said. "I wonder if my landlady knows what happened."

"If she's that lady who's staring at us from the shop window, then I'd say she does." Stella pointed to the storefront, and the wizened face that was peering out from it.

"Lucille!" Quinn called as she tried to get out of the SUV.

Tried and failed, because Stella grabbed Malone's jacket and yanked her back. "Hold your horses, Quinn. What if the guy who tried to run you down is waiting around for another opportunity?"

"Malone and Chance were going after him."

"Going after him doesn't mean they have him." She got out of the SUV, slammed the door shut and strode to Lucille's bakery. She knocked. Knocked again more loudly. "Ma'am?" she called. "Can you open the door?"

Poor Lucille looked as if she was going to have a coronary, her wrinkled face pressed close to the glass, her mouth gapping open as she stared at Stella.

"She doesn't open doors for strangers," Quinn

called, getting out of the vehicle, and ignoring Stella's hard look.

"You think she's going to open it if someone takes a potshot at you while we're walking to the door?"

"No one is going to—"

The door flew open and Lucille ran as fast as her eighty-year-old legs could carry her. She threw herself into Quinn's arms, sobbing hysterically.

"Quinn, thank goodness! I've been worried sick!"

"Didn't Sheriff Lock tell you I was okay?"

"You know how the police are," Lucille said with a quiet sniff. "They tell you what you want to hear."

"Well, he told you the truth this time. I'm fine."

"But, there was—" she glanced at Stella, lowered her voice "—blood all over the floor in the apartment."

"How did you hear about that?" Stella asked, gently prodding Lucille back toward the shop, her gaze on the road, the row of buildings, the dark shadows at the edges of the trees.

"My great-nephew is a new deputy. He called me because he was worried. Thought maybe I'd been attacked. I told him I was just fine, and then I started thinking about my dear Quinn.

Who would I have to share my morning coffee with if something happened to you, dear?"

"Nothing is going to happen to me."

"It might if we don't get inside," Stella said, but her tone was softer. "Ms. Lucille, would you mind if we talk in the shop?"

"In the shop?" Lucille blinked. "Of course, we can go in the shop."

She led them inside, the scent of fresh baked bread and cinnamon rolls drifting over Quinn as she stepped across the threshold. Three generations had run the shop before Lucille. She'd told Quinn that she was the last in the line. She hadn't married, had never had children. One day, she'd sell the shop, but for now, she could still bake the breads and treats that she'd been selling for as long as she could remember.

"Sit down, girls," she said, all the tears and worry gone, her black eyes flashing with the excitement of having late-night visitors and gossip that she could spread at the next quilting bee. "I'll make some coffee and warm up some pumpkin bread."

"Don't go to any effort, ma'am," Stella said.

"Effort? Is it effort to take a breath of morning air?" Lucille patted one of the old booths that she'd reupholstered in the seventies. Green plaid with hints of gold. She'd told Quinn that she didn't see any reason to change them. Her customers loved the shop's vibe.

What they really loved was Lucille.

"Wow!" Stella whispered as Lucille bustled into the kitchen. "She's really something. This whole shop is really something."

Quinn guessed it was, but she'd grown used to it over the years—the bright booths and the dark wood floor, the old glass display cases and the newer baskets and warming racks behind them. The old-fashioned register that Lucille still used to ring up customers—its beautiful mahogany and brass exterior a work of art.

"It's a special place," Quinn said, as Lucille reappeared, a pretty porcelain chocolate pot on a large tray, silver plates filled with breads and sweets beside it.

Quinn took the tray from her hands, placed it on the old tabletop. "This looks lovely, Lucille," she said.

"Food should always look lovely, my de…" Her voice trailed off, her eyes widening, as she opened her mouth. Tried to speak.

"Lucille!" Quinn rushed to her side, terrified she was having a heart attack.

"The window! He's in the window!" Lucille shrieked.

Stella was up like a flash, shoving Quinn to-

ward the back of the shop. "In the kitchen! Go!
Stay away from the windows and door."

"But—"

"Go!" Stella ordered, turning toward the window, a gun suddenly in her hand. "If there's a
phone, call... Never mind."

The tension eased from her body, she tucked
the gun away.

"Those idiots," she said, but there was a note
of affection in her voice, a hint of relief.

She strode to the door and yanked it open,
Lucille shrieking for her to stop or they'd all
end up dead at the hands of a murdering fiend.

Only it wasn't a murdering fiend who walked
in. It was Malone, dark hair a little mussed,
T-shirt still stained with soot, a gun holster
strapped over his chest. He looked better than
any man should, and seeing him there made
Quinn's heart do a couple little flips that had
nothing to do with fear or worry, and everything
to do with Malone.

"Well!" Lucille said, apparently realizing
Malone wasn't intent on doing any of them
bodily harm. "Perhaps next time you could
knock on the door instead of staring in the window, young man."

"My apologies, ma'am. I saw the light and
thought my friends might be inside. I didn't
mean to scare the tar out of you."

"Scare the tar, huh? Are you a Southern boy?"

"Tennessee. Born and bred."

"I've always had a soft spot for Southern manners. Sit down. We were having refreshments."

"Actually—"

"Sit! I'll bring another plate."

She hurried back to the kitchen.

"She might want to bring three more plates," Malone said. "August and Chance are talking to the sheriff. They'll be in when they finish."

"I'll go tell her," Stella offered, following Lucille into the kitchen.

And then Quinn was alone with the only guy besides Cory who'd ever made her pulse leap and her heart jump.

She ran her hand along one of the booths, avoiding his dark gaze. "Were you able to catch the guy?"

"We weren't, but a couple of deputy sheriffs snagged him off the boat he stole."

"He stole a boat?"

"Rowed out into the lake, and then realized he had nowhere to go."

"So, that's one less person going after Tabitha."

"Going after you," he corrected. "You keep forgetting that. You're a means to an end, Quinn.

Jarrod wants his wife back, and you're his way to do that now that Jubilee is inaccessible."

"I haven't forgotten, but I've got a lot of people working to keep me safe. Tabitha is on her own."

"By her own choice." He moved close, touched her chin, urging her to look into his eyes.

And how could she not?

He'd stepped into her life as a stranger, done everything he could to keep her safe. She owed him.

"Does it matter if it's her choice?" she asked softly, because her throat was tight again with that same feeling of anticipation and sorrow that she felt every time she looked into his eyes. "I still don't want her fighting this on her own."

"Because she's your sister, and you love her. Sometimes, though, we have to let the people we love learn from their mistakes."

"Learning from her mistakes might mean she dies, Malone."

"No. It won't, because we're going to prove that Jarrod is coming after her. The guy who's being booked on assault is Charles Libby, and according to the two other men who are in custody, he knows who's footing the bill for all of this. We're hoping that he'll decide to plea bargain for a lesser sentence."

"That might be difficult if he's the one who murdered the guy they found in the lake."

"Whether he did or not isn't our problem to worry about. The sheriff will handle the investigation. What I'm worried about is you." He touched her jaw, his finger skimming over the bruised skin, his eyes so filled with compassion and concern she glanced away. "I want you to go back to DC with Chance, Quinn," he said quietly. "He needs to leave in the morning so that he can be back there for Boone. We can get you a flight out, too. You can stay with him until this blows over."

"What? You're kidding, right?" He didn't look as if he was kidding. He looked dead serious.

"The three of us discussed it on the way over here, and—"

"You didn't include me in the discussion? You didn't think I'd have an opinion about what I wanted to do?"

"I knew you'd have an opinion. That's why I'm filling you in now, before your brother arrives and tries to force you to do something you don't want to do."

"How is that different from what you're doing?"

"This isn't forcing, Quinn. This is explaining. You're in danger here, and you'll continue to be in danger until Tabitha decides to seek the help she obviously needs."

"I know."

"Do you also know that it would really bother me if something happened to you?" he asked. "Do you understand that the world isn't going to be nearly as nice of a place without you in it?"

"Malone…" She shook her head, turning to look at one of the black-and-white photos that lined the wall. Pictures of the bakery when it was new, the customers wearing long dresses and hats, the men in snazzy suites and shiny shoes.

Sometimes she wished things didn't have to change, that time didn't have to march on the way it did. Sometimes, like when Cory had just been diagnosed and his health was still good, she wanted time to stand still, things to stay exactly the way they were.

There were other times, though, when she understood how wonderful it was to grow and change as time swirled around her. Like when she'd finally gotten her college degree, finally said I do, finally kissed Cory goodbye for the last time and watched him slip from suffering into eternity.

And, maybe, like now, when a man she admired seemed to admire her, and when she thought that maybe she could accept that.

"What is it?" Malone said, turning her so that they were face-to-face, ignoring Stella and Lucille who were walking back into the room, discussing the best recipe for yeast dough.

"I understand, but I can't go until I know she's okay. I can't."

He nodded, his jaw tight, his expression grim.

He didn't try to convince her, though, didn't say another word as the door opened and August walked in with Chance.

August pushed hard to get Quinn to leave. She refused. Once. Twice. A dozen times while everyone sat at the booth eating sweet bread and drinking coffee.

Finally, Malone had had all he could take. He'd spent most of his teen years listening to siblings squabble, he didn't plan to spend any more of his adult life doing the same.

"Enough," he said, interrupting August midsentence.

"What do you mean *enough*?"

"She's not leaving town. Obviously nothing you say is going to convince her to do it. The best thing any of us can do is bed down for the night, get some rest, and come at the problem fresh in the morning."

"The *problem* is Tabitha's, and I say we let

her deal with the mess she made on her own."
August paced across the room.

"I can't lose both my sisters over this," he
continued. "And if things escalate the way they
have been, that's exactly what might happen."

"You're not going to lose either of them, if
we have anything to do with it." Stella touched
his arm, and Chance frowned.

"We're *not* going to lose anyone, but we're
also not going to accomplish any more tonight."
He stood. "Let's see if we can find a place to
stay. I think there's a bed-and-breakfast in town.
If not there, then—"

"Don't be silly!" Lucille exclaimed. The
woman looked like she was ninety and acted
like she was twenty-four, bustling around on
spindly legs that didn't look as if they could hold
a toddler up. "You're not going to pay a dime to
that old bat who owns the bed-and-breakfast."

"Lucille!" Quinn chided. "Mary isn't an old
bat. She's not even sixty."

"And she doesn't care squat about that property. You know it, and I do, too. Which isn't the
point. The point is, there is no reason for any of
you to pay for a place to stay. I have plenty of
room at my house."

"We couldn't put you out like that, ma'am,"
Malone said, not because they really couldn't

but because the danger seemed to be following Quinn, and he didn't want Lucille to get hurt.

"Put me out? Are you kidding? This is the most fun I've had in decades!" Lucille sighed happily, and Malone almost felt bad for refusing.

Almost.

"We really do appreciate the offer, but there's been some trouble…"

"Like the blood, right? Someone was murdered upstairs? And you're worried the murderer will come after me while I'm sleeping because I've given you all a place to stay?" She shook her head, white curls bouncing wildly. "It's a sad, sick world we live in, but don't worry, I've watched plenty of true-crime shows. I know how these things work. I'll keep my bear spray under my pillow and spray any intruder who enters my boudoir in the face."

Someone snorted.

Maybe August. It was hard to tell because he'd turned away and was staring at the floor.

"Lucille," Chance said, taking both her hands in his, turning on the charm the way Malone had seen him do countless times before. "We appreciate your willingness to sacrifice your safety for us, but my organization is built on the premise that we never draw someone into an unsafe situation unless it is absolutely necessary. Tonight, it isn't. We can rest in the SUV—"

"You'll stay here, then!" Lucille interrupted, her cheeks pink. "I'll just drive over to the house and get some pillows and blankets. This young lady can come with me." She grabbed Stella's hand and started dragging her to the door. "You can sleep on the benches or the floor. Not the most comfortable arrangements, but better than the Blue Bonnet. Besides, I may not like Mary, but I certainly don't want her dead."

Stella paused at the door, met Chance's eyes. He nodded his approval of the plan, and she disappeared, dragged out into the darkness by a woman who was two inches shorter and about twenty pounds lighter than she was.

"Man!" August said. "That woman must have been something when she was young."

"She's still something," Quinn said, grabbing plates and empty coffee cups and piling them onto a tray. "I'm going to wash these."

She hurried from the room, and Malone had the distinct impression that she was running away.

From him?

From her brother?

From the pressure people had been putting on her? She'd held fast in her refusal to leave town, but he'd seen her wavering, seen how tired she was getting.

And why wouldn't she be tired?

She'd been running nonstop since Tabitha had handed Jubilee over to her.

"You going to check on her?" August said casually. "Or should I?"

"I will."

"Before you go—" August stepped in front of him, blocking his path to the kitchen "—I'm going to tell you right now that I don't want my sister hurt."

"That's what we're working to avoid." He didn't much like having his way blocked, but since August was Quinn's brother he didn't push him out of the way or try to step around him.

"You know what I'm talking about, Malone," August growled. "So don't try to be a smart aleck."

"He doesn't have to try," Chance said. "Being a smart aleck is his natural state of being. So is being excellent at his job, so how about you step out of the way before he decides to take you down, and I let him?"

"I'd like to see him try," August said.

"For the record," Malone said, forcing his voice to be calm, his tone conciliatory, "I don't hurt people I care about, and for the record, I care about your sister."

August frowned, all the anger draining from his face.

"Way to make me feel like a loser, man,"

he mumbled, moving to the side and letting Malone pass.

He walked into a large kitchen. An old-fashioned oven took up most of one wall, bread warmers on either side of it. A larger industrial oven stood on the other side of the room, a long marble island between them. There was a walk-in freezer, an open pantry filled with ingredients, a stainless steel counter with a wide sink.

Quinn stood there, her back to Malone, his jacket still dwarfing her small frame. She'd pushed up the sleeves, and he could see the narrowness of her wrists, the delicacy of her bones.

She knew he was there.

Her shoulders tensed as he moved across the room, but she didn't turn from the pile of dishes or the sudsy water she'd shoved her hands into.

"What's wrong, Quinn?" he asked. "The truth. Not some pretty lie about being worried about your sister."

"I *am* worried about my sister," she mumbled, and he realized she was crying, her voice muffled by her tears.

He urged her around, used a clean dish towel to dry her cheeks and then her hands. He'd known a lot of women in his life, and he'd dated more than a few, but he'd never wanted to understand anyone as much as he wanted to understand Quinn. "So, why the tears?"

"I don't know."

"Don't know or don't want to say?"

"A little of both." She offered a shaky laugh, turned back to the sink. "When my husband first got sick, we knew how limited his time might be."

He moved in beside her, nudging her over so he could rinse the dishes after she washed them. He didn't speak, just waited for her to finish whatever it was she wanted to say.

"I was thinking a little bit ago, that I wanted that time to go on forever, because he was feeling good, and it seemed like if we could just hold on to those moments everything would be okay," she continued, handing him a plate. "But, no matter how much I wished time to stand still, it just kept on moving forward. Then he got sicker and sicker, and I wanted time to fly by because I knew he was suffering and there was nothing we could do, no way to change the trajectory he was on. I just wanted him to be at peace."

"I think most people would feel the same."

"Maybe. I'm only me, and I can't speak for anyone else. It's difficult to watch someone you love suffer. I knew he'd be in Heaven when he died, that he'd be whole and healthy and happy, and I knew it was what he wanted, that it was my selfishness that made me want him to hang

around a few more days or hours or minutes."
She finished the last dish, handed it to him, her
gray eyes dark with fatigue. "The thing is, log-
ically I know that Cory would want me to be
happy, too. That he'd never want me to spend
my life mourning him, but it's hard moving on."

"Wouldn't it be harder to stay in the same
place?" he asked gently, and she nodded.

"Yes, but I'm moving slowly, Malone. Time
is just kind of creeping along, and I don't want
to rush it, because everything feels new, and I
feel a little…" She shrugged and tucked a strand
of hair behind her ear. "I don't know how I feel.
Except that I'm twenty-eight, and starting all
this again." She gestured to him and to herself.

"I just told your brother, I never hurt people
I care about. I also never rush them. We have
all the time in the world, Quinn." He traced the
line of her jaw, ran his thumb across the pulse
point in her neck, feeling the rapid throb of her
heartbeat.

"Quinn!" August shouted, and she jumped,
a nervous laugh bursting out.

"Not if August has anything to do with it."

"Your brother has issues," he muttered, and
she laughed again, the sounded lighter and easier as she grabbed his hand and tugged him back
into the service area.

THIRTEEN

Lucille brought enough blankets and pillows to provide every citizen of Echo Lake a comfortable place to sleep.

At least, that's the way it seemed to Quinn as she lay on a thick padding of blankets and sheets and stared up at the shop's ceiling. The room was quiet, just the soft sound of breathing from the three people who weren't on guard duty breaking the silence.

Chance was somewhere in the kitchen, keeping his ears and eyes open for trouble. No one seemed to think there'd be any. It helped that the sheriff had parked at the curb outside of the shop. Only a fool would try to get in, and Quinn didn't think Jarrod was that. The fact that he hadn't returned Stella's call seemed to make everyone think that he was still out of the country. Maybe he was. Quinn hoped that he was, but there was something nagging at the back of her mind. That Post-it note on the photo album page. The man in the picture who hadn't been in any other photo in the book. Nothing? Something?

She didn't know, but she couldn't shake the feeling that she needed to look at it more carefully, try a little harder to figure out why her sister had stuck a Post-it note on that page.

She eased up from her heavy down comforter, trying to move quietly enough not to disturb anyone. She'd ask Chance to retrieve the backpack, and then she'd sit in the kitchen and look through it, really study all the pages, try to decipher any message her sister might have been sending.

"Flying the coop?" Malone asked quietly as she stood.

"I thought you were asleep," she whispered.

"I could say the same about you."

"And I could say that I wish the two of you would shut up, but I don't think it would do any good," Stella grumbled.

"What's going on?" August muttered.

"I was thinking about the backpack Tabitha left for Jubilee."

"That little pink one?" Stella sat up, apparently wide-awake and ready for whatever would come.

"Yes."

"What about it?"

Quinn explained quickly, and Stella stood. "Well, that's it. None of us are going to be able to get back to sleep until we know what's going on with the picture. I'll get the backpack. You want to tell Chance, Malone?"

"Tell me what?" Chance flipped on the light, and everyone was moving, heading for the door or into the kitchen, grabbing coffee cups and pouring some from the pot Lucille had insisted on brewing before she left. An hour ago? Two?

By the time, Stella returned with the backpack, the group was sipping coffee and the sheriff had joined them, his long legs spread out under one of the tables, his fingers tapping against the tabletop.

"You're sure the Post-it note had your name on it, Quinn?" he asked, and she nodded, reaching into the pack and pulling out the small book.

It was a baby album, the cover stained and worn, a picture of a red-haired infant glued into a cardboard oval cutout on the front.

Chance whistled softly when he saw it, touching the photo and then snapping a picture of it with his phone. "I've seen that photo before. Boone has the same one in his wallet."

"I guess the album has been with Jubilee all along, then," Quinn said. Imagining Jubilee's mother pasting that photo into the album made her heart ache, and she opened the book, turning to the page that had been marked with the Post-it note.

The photo was still there—the older man staring out at her, his eyes such a light blue they looked nearly translucent.

"Wonder who that is?" Malone said, leaning in, his arm brushing hers.

She'd said a lot to him in the kitchen. Too much, maybe, but she didn't regret it. She'd learned a lot of things from her father. Most of them about how she didn't want to be. No games. Ever. That's the way she lived her life. Malone made her feel things she hadn't felt in a long, long time, and she wasn't going to pretend it wasn't true, she wasn't going to try to hide it.

"I have no idea." She opened the clear plastic pocket that contained the photo, slid the picture out.

Something dropped onto the table. A folded up piece of newspaper that Malone picked up.

"Do you mind?" he asked, and she shook her head.

"Go ahead."

He unfolded it, frowned. "It's dated a month ago. An article about a suicide in Las Vegas."

"Whose suicide?" Sheriff Lock asked.

"Based on the photo in the paper, I'd say it's the guy who's in that picture." Malone lay the newspaper down, smoothing the folds to reveal a black-and-white photo of a man who looked remarkably similar to the one in the picture Quinn was holding.

"John Engle," Sheriff Lock said, as if somehow saying it would help them all understand exactly who the man was and why his photo was in Jubilee's album.

"Hold on," Malone said, lifting the article again. "This says he was a real estate broker, partner to—"

"Let me guess," Chance broke in. "Jarrod Williams."

"Exactly." Malone smiled, his lips curving, his eyes predatory and hard. "Messy suicide, too. His wife found him in his bathtub at home. He bled to death."

"Slit wrists?" Stella asked.

"Probably. The article doesn't say. There were drugs in his system, though. Prescription pain killers, antidepressants."

"A note?" Chance asked.

"Not that the article mentions."

"It sounds like the guy had problems," August cut in. "But I'm not sure what that has to do with Tabitha or her husband."

"This kind of suicide is one of the easiest to stage," Stella remarked. "You drug the guy, strip him down, toss him in a tub and slit his wrists."

"That's a very cold way to say it," Quinn said,

shuddering at the thought of someone being so calculating, so cruel as to plan a murder that would make the victim look like the perpetrator.

"Not cold. Factual. I saw it once or twice during my time in the navy. A spouse fed up with his or her marriage, deciding that the easiest way to end things was to get rid of the person they were tired of. Of course, no one wants to get caught, so the smart ones? They try to make someone else look guilty. Suicide is the perfect cover, *if* you can make it look authentic."

"If that's the case this time, the perp was successful. There's no mention of an investigation, no indication that the police were suspicious." Malone pulled out his phone. "I'm going to call the Las Vegas police department. They might be able to tell us more."

"I'll do that," Sheriff Lock responded. "They'll be more open to a fellow police officer."

"What's interesting to me," Stella remarked, her gaze on the article, "is the quote from the guy's widow. She says she got home from a shopping trip to New York and found him in the bathroom. The walls and floor were splattered with blood. It takes a lot of force to cut into a major artery. Most people are too scared and too pain sensitive to do it. Which is why most suicide attempts like this one aren't fatal."

"He did have prescription drugs in his system," Chance said.

"Which would make it even less likely that he'd be effective at cutting that deeply."

"Maybe the wife was exaggerating," August suggested. "It happens. People get into traumatic situations, and what they remember isn't always what happened."

"If she wasn't," Malone remarked, "anyone in the room with him would have been splattered with blood, too. Or am I overreaching there, Stella?"

"If a major artery was hit, people in the vicinity would be splattered. That's the way it is." She set the article down. "So, the question is, did he do it to himself, or did someone help him along?"

"I'd say someone." August lifted the album, thumbed through it. "And I'd guess it was this guy right here." He jabbed at a photo of a handsome man holding a red-haired baby.

"Jarrod Williams." Malone nodded. "They were in business together. Maybe something happened to cause a rift. Money missing. Something underhanded that John found out about and didn't like. He might have threatened to go to the authorities."

"So, Jarrod killed him. Made it look like a suicide, and somehow Tabitha found out?" August raked a hand through his hair, shook his head. "If that's all true, she should have gone to the police."

"You think they would have believed her?" Quinn asked. "You're her brother, and you didn't."

"I know." He stood. "And I'm sorry for that."

"How about we just slow down a little?" Sheriff Lock suggested. "We can't assume a crime was committed unless there's evidence pointing toward it. I'm going to make a couple of calls. I'll keep you posted on what I find out. In the meantime, we'll keep working on our newest guest at the county jail. See if we can get him to tell us who's paying his bills."

"He's still not talking?" Malone asked.

"No, but he may change his mind once we start questioning him about the body we found in the lake. Turns out, he and the deceased were buddies way back in high school. I don't think it's coincidence that they ended up in Echo Lake at the same time." He walked to the door, pulled it open. "Stay alert, and call if you hear from your sister, Quinn. Our goal is to help her, and you can let her know that."

"I will." Not that Tabitha would have any way to reach Quinn. Neither of them had cell phones.

She wanted to hear from her sister, though. She wanted to know that she was safe, and then she wanted to tell Tabitha to go to the police, trust that they'd listen to whatever she had to say.

Trust.

That thing that Quinn had never been good at. Yet there she sat, allowing others to make decisions, to take actions that would impact people she loved.

She frowned. She needed more coffee. More sugar. Everyone else seemed wired, the energy in the room palpable. Not Quinn, she was foggy-headed, thick-brained.

She walked into the kitchen, rinsed out the coffee pot and started a new one. She could hear voices drifting in from the service area, hear the soft whistle of wind beneath the shop's eaves. She poured a cup of coffee, sipping it as she filled a tray with mugs, sugar, cream.

The bakery phone rang, the sound so surprising it took a minute for Quinn to realize what it was. It was a strange time for someone to be calling to place an order, but Lucille was old-fashioned. She didn't have an answering machine, didn't have voice mail. She answered the phone when she was there, let it ring when she wasn't.

The last ring cut off abruptly.

The phone began ringing again almost immediately.

Whoever it was must be desperate.

Quinn grabbed the tablet Lucille wrote orders on and answered the phone.

"Hello?"

Nothing but silence, and then a quiet sob.

"Tabitha?" she asked, her heart beating hard in her chest.

"No," someone responded, the words muffled with tears. "It's me. The bear spray didn't work, Quinn. He got me, and he says if you don't come alone—"

"I will kill her," someone else finished, the voice masculine, polished and very, very cold. "Do you understand what I'm saying to you?"

"Yes." She managed to speak through the cotton that seemed to have filled her mouth.

"You come to the old lady's house. We'll do an even exchange. You for her."

"Who is this?"

"If you want to see your friend alive again, I guess you'll come to her house and find out. You have fifteen minutes to make it here. Alone, Quinn. If I see anyone else with you, the old lady dies. If you don't get here on time, you'll both die. That's my promise to you, and I never, ever break a promise." He hung up, and she was left standing there, the phone in her hand, her pulse racing, her thoughts racing.

"Everything okay in here?" Malone asked, and she turned to face him, knew she had a choice to make—do what she'd been told to do, or trust Malone with the truth.

She hesitated, looked into his dark eyes, thought about the things he'd told her, the man he'd proved himself to be.

"No," she finally said, and then she told him everything.

Fifteen minutes was enough time to brew a pot of coffee. It was enough time to run a couple of miles. It was enough time to do a lot of things, but it wasn't enough time to come up with a plan that would free Lucille and keep Quinn safe.

The perp knew that.

Malone knew it, too, and he wasn't happy. Not when Stella suggested that they let Quinn approach the old Victorian from the front while the team moved in from the back. Not when Chance agreed it was their only option. Not when August hopped on board and volunteered to do recon—going in ahead of the team, to find the easiest route into the house. He'd left twelve minutes before the deadline, had checked in when he reached the house, describing the woods that butted up against the back of the property, the wide expanse of yard that would have to be crossed to access the large Victorian. A window on the lower level was open.

Maybe even broken. August was too far away to see, but he thought they'd be able to gain entrance there.

Even Sheriff Lock seemed happy with the plan.

He'd called in deputies to block off entrances to the street. Every one of them had walked in on foot, setting down traffic cones and spike strips designed to slow down fleeing vehicles.

Everything was in place.

Every*one* was in place.

All of them waiting for Malone to do his part—walk Quinn to the end of the road, make sure she was clear on every aspect of the plan.

"Four minutes," he heard Stella say through the earpiece he was wearing.

"Got it," he growled, all his frustration and fear seeping into those words.

He did not want to do this—walk Quinn to the end of the road, send her into a blind situation with an unknown aggressor.

Who was he kidding?

He didn't want to send her in anywhere. If he'd had his way, Stella would have gone in as a decoy, but he'd been voted down, the possibility that Lucille would be killed if the perp realized he was being tricked a very real one.

"Do not enter the house," he reminded Quinn,

the words ringing hollowly in the still night air.
"You're going in as a distraction so that—"

"The team can get in the back of the house
and rescue Lucille," she finished wearily. "I
think we've been over this a dozen times."

"And we'll go over it a dozen more."

"No." She stopped, touched his arm. "We
won't, because we're out of time, and this is
where we're supposed to part ways."

"I'm as aware of that as you are of the plan,"
he said, dragging her closer, whispering so only
she could hear. "You don't have to do this. The
team can go in without you."

"I do have to do it, because without me at
the front of the house, he's going to hear what's
going on in the back. Then he's going to do
what he promised and kill Lucille, and I'm never
going to forgive myself for that."

"Quinn—"

"And you wouldn't forgive yourself, either,
Malone. You know it."

It was true.

He couldn't risk Lucille, and he didn't want
to risk Quinn. It was a no-win situation.

God is still in control.

Those words, another motto to live by.

He brushed his lips against Quinn's, the touch
gentle and light but filled with dozens of words
that he didn't have time to say—*be careful, I*

need you to come back to me. Do exactly what
we planned. Don't take chances.

"Two minutes." Stella's warning was so loud,
Quinn heard.

She jumped back, her hand flying to her
mouth.

"I won't say I'm sorry," he told her.

"I wouldn't want you to. See you soon," she
said, and it sounded like a promise, like a hope,
like something she wanted desperately to believe in.

He watched as she rounded the street corner,
her shadow bouncing in the street light. She was
jogging, hurrying to make it in the allotted time.
Her friend's life was on the line, and she was
willing to risk anything to save it.

He admired that.

He'd have done the same.

But he didn't like it.

"One," Stella said, a note of panic in her
voice. "Don't mess this up because your heart
is involved, Malone. If you do, I'll never let you
live it down."

"She's on the way," he responded. "So am I,"
he added, and then he sprinted into the woods
that edged the street and made his way toward
Lucille's property.

FOURTEEN

The last time Quinn had been this terrified, she'd been sitting in an oncologist's office listening to the doctor diagnose her husband.

Cancer. Inoperable.

Her heart had pounded harder with every word, a fast, sickening beat that had almost drowned out what was being said.

Six months.

Maybe a year.

The doctor had been somber, filling the awful silences with words that were supposed to take the sting out of the diagnosis.

There's always hope.

She'd wanted to believe that Cory would be the exception to the rule, but she'd felt sick with dread, certain that everything she'd dreamed of, everything she'd hoped for was about to be taken from her. She'd left the office knowing what was facing them—months of treatment,

months of struggle, months of watching someone she loved suffer.

She hadn't known how helpless she would
feel, though. Hadn't understood the depth of
despair that came with knowing she couldn't
help the person she loved most.

She felt the same despair now, the same terror. Only there was a different kind of horror
waiting for her. Not the slow suffering of someone she loved. Lucille's death would be quick
and brutal, and it would be all Quinn's fault.

Fear or not, Quinn had to do this.

She sprinted up the road, cutting through a
neighbor's yard as she made her way to Lucille's
Victorian house. The place was huge, meant to
be filled with a family. Instead, Lucille lived
there alone, her cat, Kitty, her only companion.

Sad. And sadder to think she might die there
at the hands of a man who wanted...

What?

Tabitha?

Quinn pounded across the yard, not stopping
when the security lights went on. She was at
the top of the porch stairs when she heard her
name. Not the quiet whisper that had drifted
from the churchyard. This was a full-out yell
filled with panic.

"Quinn! No!"

Quinn turned, saw someone racing across the street.

Blond hair shining in the darkness, slim frame still dressed in a fitted suit.

Tabitha! Running straight toward her, still screaming Quinn's name.

"Don't—" Quinn started, but the door to the house flew open.

She heard it. Felt someone rushing outside.

She tried to run, but hard hands grabbed her waist, yanking her back toward the open door.

Tabitha was still in the yard, frozen there.

Quinn was too busy fighting to do more than scream for her to run.

She jabbed an elbow into rock-hard abs, stepped on a foot. Kicked a shin.

"Stop," the man growled, snagging one of her arms, and yanking it up behind her back. Pain shot through her shoulder and up into her jaw. She stilled, trying to ease the pain, trying to see through the haze that seemed to be clouding her vision.

Go! Quinn wanted to yell at her sister, but she couldn't get the word out.

"There," the man crooned, his voice sending chills up her spine. "That's what I want. Just cooperate, Quinn. After all, it's the first time we've met. You should want to make a good impression on your in-law."

"You're not making a good impression on me," she said, clenching her teeth against the pain.

"Call your sister," he commanded.

"No."

He yanked her arm up higher, twisting her hand in opposition to the movement. Something in her wrist popped, the pain so intense, darkness edged in and her legs went out from under her.

"Don't!" he growled, dragging her up by the arm. "We've got a lot to do, and I don't have time to waste on swooning females. Tabitha!" he called. "You'd better get moving, because I'm not in the mood for games tonight. You keep standing there like the idiot you are, and your sister is going to die. Right here. Right now."

"Like John died?" Tabitha called. "Are you going to murder her, too?"

She was trying to buy time, Quinn was certain of it.

Did she know there were men moving in from the back of the house? Could she see something that Quinn couldn't?

"John committed suicide because he was weak," Jarrod said easily, the words well practiced and smooth.

"You killed him because he learned you were

laundering money through your casino, and he was going to turn you in."

"That's a lie. All of it."

"Is the blood on the clothes you wore the night John died a lie? You knew I found them in your gym bag, didn't you? That's why you went into a rage when I said I wanted to take a vacation. You knew I had them, but you were afraid to ask, afraid I might record the conversation and use it against you. For once, I was a step ahead of you, and you hated it."

"Shut up!" Jarrod yelled, shifting his grip, pulling something from his jacket pocket.

Quinn felt cold metal at the hollow of her throat, realized exactly what he had—a knife, the sharp blade digging into her skin.

"I tried to play nice, Tabitha. Just like I always do. You forced me to this. Get up here. *Now.* If you don't you'll see exactly what kind of damage a knife can do."

"Don't—" Quinn started, but the knife blade dug deeper, a trickle of blood sliding along her collarbone.

"*You* don't," Jarrod ordered. "Don't talk. Don't move. Don't even think about sacrificing your life for the life of your worthless sister. I gave her everything. A gorgeous house. Clothes. Jewelry. Money. She repaid me by kidnapping my child—"

"Jubilee was never yours," Tabitha said as she walked up the porch stairs. One slow step at a time, her gaze on her husband, her face so pale Quinn was surprised she was still on her feet.

"She has always been mine. Her mother gave her to me. A gift for what I gave her."

"Drugs?" Tabitha spat. "Is that what you paid her with?"

"I loved her, and I loved our child. That's a concept you can't seem to understand."

"You're wrong, Jarrod. I know what love is. I felt it for you for a long time. If I hadn't, I would have taken Jubilee to her birth father the day I found her birth certificate in the safe."

"Found because you were snooping, trying to see if there was anything you could steal."

"You gave me the combination, Jarrod. Have you forgotten that?" she asked wearily, and Quinn could see she was at her breaking point, that she was near collapse.

"I gave it to you because I figured you were too stupid to look at anything but the jewelry and the cash."

"I've never been stupid until it came to you. I really believed you loved me." There were tears in her eyes, and Quinn wanted to tell her not to cry, but one slip and the knife would cut through her throat.

Where was Malone?

The rest of the team?

Waiting it out? Trying to get a good shot?

"You never loved me, though. You wanted the things I had. That's the real reason you kept quiet about Jubilee. You knew you'd have to give all those pretty things up if you took my daughter away. Admit it!" He jabbed the blade a little deeper, warm blood oozing from the fresh cut.

Quinn didn't feel the pain from it.

She could barely feel the pulsing agony in her wrist.

She was looking at her sister, trying to read her facial expression, trying to get some clue as to what she had planned.

"I admit that's why I kept quiet at first. Later, though…" She finally looked at Quinn, offering a sad, sorry smile that made Quinn's heart ache. "I fell in love with being her mom. I realized I was my best me when I was taking care of Jubilee. I didn't want to give that up. It was selfish. I know it was, but I loved her."

"You don't love anyone," Jarrod spat, his grip on Quinn's arm loosening. "I needed a wife who would be willing to do anything for me. I needed a wife who would sacrifice her time, her energy, even her child for me! I gave you everything to ensure you would do that. And what did you do? You betrayed me. Where are the clothes I left in my gym bag, Tabitha? You locked them away somewhere, right? So you could blackmail me into giving you more money."

"I locked them away so you couldn't get your hands on them while I was bringing Jubilee to safety."

"Protecting my daughter from me? Not necessary." His voice had gone silky smooth. "You're going to pay. You know that, don't you?"

"So are you, I already called the Las Vegas police and told them where they could find the clothes. I told them that you murdered John, and I told them why. I'm not nearly as stupid as you think. I've hacked into your computer system. I found the emails you sent to John, the ones where you threatened to kill him if he went to the police."

"Exactly. I warned him that he'd pay if he crossed me. He committed suicide when he decided to betray me!"

"You're crazy," Tabitha whispered. "I cannot believe I ever loved you."

Jarrod growled, shoving Quinn forward. She landed hard, her bad wrist taking the brunt of the fall. She saw stars, heard screams. Lucille? Tabitha?

Quinn rolled to her side, saw her sister at the bottom of the porch stairs, Jarrod grasping her hair, slamming her head into the pavement.

"No!" Quinn scrambled to her feet, her stomach heaving as pain shot through her arm. It didn't matter. Nothing mattered except Tabitha.

She lunged down the stairs, slamming into Jarrod. He tumbled sideways, and Quinn grabbed Tabitha's hand, tried to pull her to her feet.

"Get up!" she shouted. "Tabitha!"

But her sister's eyes were closed, blood seeping from beneath her head, soaking into the green grass, staining the earth.

"This is ending. Now!" Jarrod shouted, and he was up again, moving toward them, the knife raised.

The air exploded with sound, the night reverberating with it.

The knife dropped from Jarrod's hand, and he fell to the ground, howling with rage and with pain.

Shadows moved in.

No. Not shadows. Men. Women.

Stella touched Quinn's arm, murmuring something about her being tougher than Stella had given her credit for. She was there. Then gone. And Quinn thought maybe she'd imagined the whole thing. Maybe there weren't deputies rushing toward her. Maybe August wasn't bounding down the porch stairs.

"You okay, sis?" he said.

"Yes," she mumbled.

"You're bleeding."

"Tabitha is hurt worse. You need to help her." She got the words out, and he moved past her, kneeling next to their sister's still form.

Sirens screamed, and the sheriff was suddenly striding across the yard.

He yanked Jarrod to his feet, and Quinn could see that her sister's husband had already been handcuffed, his right hand seeping blood. No one seemed worried about his injury. She supposed that meant he was going to live.

Quinn wasn't sure how she felt about that.

She wasn't sure how she felt about anything.

Her legs buckled, and she would have gone down, but an arm slid around her waist, warm fingers caressed her side.

"It's okay," Malone said, easing her to the ground. "Everything is okay."

"Lucille?"

"Right here," Chance said as he led Lucille out onto the porch. She had her hair in curlers, a plastic shower cap covering them.

"Quinn!" she said, her voice trembling. "I was terrified for you! Are you okay?"

"I was terrified for you, too," Quinn mumbled, the words seeming to trip all over themselves. She felt shaky and disconnected, not sure what was real and what was imagination.

Lucille patted her shower cap, zipped her

housecoat a little tighter. "Oh, my. The neighbors are coming out, and I'm standing here like this. Young man!" She patted Chance's arm. "Bring me back inside so I can make myself presentable."

"I'm not sure that the sheriff wants you in the house, ma'am."

"Do I look like I give a lick what the sheriff wants?" She hooked her arm through Chance's, dragged him back into the house.

Quinn wanted to smile, but her face felt numb. Her body felt numb. As a matter of fact, she wasn't sure if she was sitting or standing.

"Whoa!" Malone said, his arm tightening on her waist. "You got through the worst of it. Don't pass out on me now, Quinn."

"I won't," she said, but the world was going dark, everything around her fading.

The last thing she saw were Malone's eyes— those beautiful dark eyes—and then she saw nothing at all.

Three stitches on her collar bone and a cast on her wrist. Things could have gone a lot worse for Quinn, but in Malone's mind they could have gone a lot better. The team had been at the back of the house, everything going exactly the way they'd planned it when they'd heard Tabitha calling for Quinn. She'd been the surprise player, the heroine who no one would have ever suspected of heroism.

They'd been wrong.

They'd underestimated Tabitha, and both women had almost died because of it. That didn't sit well. At all.

Malone scowled, pacing Quinn's hospital room. She looked dead to the world, her face pale, her bruise deep purple and blue. A bandage peeked out from her hospital gown, the edge of it just visible. A thick red scratch snacked out from under it, the end of it right over her jugular.

She could have died.

The thought infuriated him.

But Chance had been right. They'd both already crawled through the window when Jarrod made his move, and Malone had raced through the house, nearly run onto the porch.

Chance had held him back, told him to wait it out, take an opportunity when it presented itself and not before.

It had been one of the toughest things Malone had ever had to do—watch from the shadows while Quinn was terrorized. If he'd acted sooner, though, the knife would have plunged deeper, might have arched higher, and she might have bled to death before help arrived.

He'd waited, and then he'd moved, lunging through the front door as Quinn tried to save her sister. Another heartbeat of waiting to make sure she wasn't going to get into his line of sight, and then he'd taken aim, shot Jarrod's knife hand.

He'd almost aimed at the guy's heart, but taking a life was always a last resort. Offering mercy in this case? Harder than with others. Jarrod was crazy. There'd been no doubt about that. He'd ranted and raved all the way to the sheriff's car, and Malone was certain he'd done the same all the way to jail. Worse, though, he'd been bent on killing. He was determined to take Tabitha out and to take Quinn out with her. A bullet to the heart didn't seem like unfair punishment. But then, there'd been plenty of times in Malone's life when he hadn't gotten the punishment he'd deserved, when he'd been granted clemency, given mercy instead of justice.

Jarrod would stand trial eventually, and it would be up to a jury to decide his guilt or innocence. More than likely, he'd go to jail for the rest of his life.

"And he deserves it," he muttered, checking his phone messages for what seemed like the hundredth time. Nothing from Chance. He must have made his flight out. He'd be in DC in a couple of hours, meeting with Boone and his wife to offer the support they needed.

"Who deserves what?" Quinn said sluggishly, her words slurred.

"You're awake." He moved to her side, lifted her good hand. Her skin was smooth and soft, her hand dry and warm and filled with life. He'd come *this* close to losing her. The thought shook him to the core.

"And you're pacing like a caged tiger," she replied. "Now that we've established that, *who deserves what*?"

"Jarrod deserves to spend the rest of his life in jail."

"He's there now, right?" Her gaze shot to the door as if she were afraid Tabitha's husband might burst through it.

"Yes," he assured her. "He's locked away. For good. The best lawyers in the world couldn't get him a Get Out of Jail Free card.

"Good." She closed her eyes, and he thought she might have drifted off again. "Funny," she continued, opening her eyes again, "I thought I saw the sheriff take Jarrod away, but everything is kind of hazy, and the memories just won't seem to stick. Except…"

"Jarrod and his knife?"

"No," she laughed shakily. "You. Your eyes, I mean. You have beautiful eyes."

"I think the medicine is getting to you, Quinn."

"You're getting to me. That kiss got to me."

He laughed, tucking a strand of hair behind her ear, and skimming her cheek with his
knuckles. "You're going to be very upset with
yourself later."

"For telling the truth?"

"For letting me know what the truth is."

"No. I won't," she said, suddenly stone-cold
sober. No slurred words. So sluggish speech. If
the medicine had been affecting her, it didn't
seem to be anymore. "One thing I learned from
watching my husband battle cancer—we only
get one chance to walk this path. If we don't
take the opportunities that come our way, we
may never get them again."

"Am I your opportunity?" he asked, smoothing her hair, his heart filled with a hundred
dreams he hadn't realized he wanted.

Until now. Until Quinn.

"I think you are," she whispered, and there
were tears in her eyes and on her cheeks.

He wiped them away, his palm smoothing
over velvety skin. "Then why are you crying?"

"Because, I didn't think I'd have an opportunity like this again. I didn't think I'd want one."

"And you're sorry that you do?"

"I'm not sorry for anything that has to do with
you, Malone." She touched his cheek, her fingers tracing the line of his scar. He sat down on
the edge of the bed so he could cradle her in his

arms. She fit perfectly there, her head against his chest, her arm around his waist.

"But, you're still crying," he pointed out, wiping tears from her cheeks.

"It's hard to see something end. Even when what I'm beginning is so wonderful."

"I'm sorry, Quinn." There was nothing else he could say. No other comfort he could offer. She'd lost someone she loved. Because of that, they'd found each other.

"Don't be. I'm where I'm supposed to be. All the tough stuff? It led me here. And Cory? He'd be happy for me. He'd have liked you, Malone. I know he would have."

"I'm pretty sure I'd have liked him, too."

"Yeah?" she said with a soft smile, and he kissed her forehead, her cheek, let his lips taste hers. Just a brief touch. A comforting one.

"Yeah. Now, how about I call your brother and tell him that you're awake? He's been texting me nonstop."

"Where is he?"

"The Portland trauma center. That's where they took Tabitha."

The words must have sparked Quinn's memory.

She shoved the blankets and sheets away, tried to stand. "Tabitha! I can't believe that I'm sitting here blubbering about my life when her husband nearly murdered her!"

"Slow down," he commanded. "You don't want to open your stitches up."

"My sister is at a trauma center, Malone. She could be dying, and I'm sitting on a hospital bed, doing nothing about it. My stitches are the least of my worries!"

"She was bleeding a lot, but it's a superficial wound. She hit her head on a rock."

"*He* hit her head on a rock," she corrected him. "I saw him do it."

"And now he's in jail, and your sister's head is stitched up, and your brother is at the hospital taking care of her."

"I'm surprised. Those two have never gotten along."

"Your brother knows how to come through when he has to."

She frowned. "Did you talk him into it?"

"I explained my thoughts about people who don't take care of their families. Truthfully, I don't think he needed to hear them. He might not trust Tabitha, but he does care about her."

It was a mild version of what happened, but he wasn't going to tell Quinn that. August had some hang-ups. Just like everyone. Eventually, he'd work through them. Hopefully, Tabitha would work through hers, too, and the two of them could patch things up.

"There's more to the story," she accused, and he smiled.

"He wanted to be here for you. I told him that I could manage."

"And?"

"That's all you need to know for now. I'll tell you all the details when you're not in a hospital bed."

His phone buzzed and he glanced at it, his pulse jumping as he read the text.

"Is that August?" Quinn asked, and he shook his head.

"No. I think your brother got tired of pestering me about your health. He's been silent for a couple of hours. This is from Chance. He said Boone is going to finally see his daughter on Saturday. He and his wife, Scout, want you and your sister to be there. They think it will make the transition easier on Jubilee. Her caseworker agrees."

"Are you serious?" she said, bouncing off the bed, the hospital gown dragging on the floor as she walked to the closet and opened the door. "I need to get dressed."

"We have until Saturday, Quinn. I don't think it's going to take that long for you to put on your clothes." He laughed, and she smiled, her eyes dove gray and filled with humor.

"Probably not, but I have a lot of other things to do before then," she responded, grabbing a bag filled with her clothes and holding it up triumphantly. "Can you wait in the hall while I put these on?"

"Even if you get dressed, you can't leave the hospital," he said, but he figured he was wrong. He was pretty sure Quinn could do just about anything she set her mind to. "The doctor hasn't cleared you yet."

"No?" She smiled, rang for the nurse. "You should probably go warm up the car."

"We don't have a car. Stella drove it to the airport to drop Chance off, and she hasn't returned yet."

"Call a taxi, then," she suggested, nudging him toward the door. "The sooner I get back to my place, the sooner I can start making plans for the trip. I want to fix up the photo album, make it a little prettier. Possibly take the photos of Jarrod—"

"I have a better idea." He stopped short of the threshold, turning to pull her close. "How about we just take it slow, Quinn? You get dressed, maybe we go get something to eat in the cafeteria. We can talk about everything and nothing and all the stuff in between while we wait for Stella, okay? There will be time enough for everything else after that, and if there isn't? I guess we'll just say everything else wasn't all that important."

She blinked, a slow soft smile curving her lips. "Our first official date?"

"We have to have one sometime, don't we?"

"Yes," she said quietly, a hint of sadness in her eyes, the shadow of it mixed with joy, excitement, happiness. "We do, but not until I get dressed."

She shoved him out the door, and he went, because they had all the time in the world to find their way to the cafeteria, all the time in the world to have their first date, all the time in the world to figure out what it meant to dream together.

Together.

Yeah. He liked the sound of that.

He liked it a lot.

FIFTEEN

Spending twelve hours in the car with her siblings?

Not something Quinn had been looking forward to. Seeing Malone at the end of the journey? That was a different story. She'd been anticipating it since he'd flown home three days ago—planning her outfit, her hair, her smile.

She'd found herself practicing *that* in front of her mirror. That's when she'd realized just how far gone she was.

Very, very far.

Very, very fast.

And that scared her.

She smoothed the pretty cotton skirt Tabitha had helped her pick—light blue with tiny flowers dotting the fabric—and tried to tell herself to breathe. A few more minutes and they'd be at their destination. The Andersons' house. They'd already entered the neighborhood, the houses old and stately, the yards well-kept and mature.

"You're sure we're heading in the right direction?" Quinn asked, and August sighed.

"I was sure the last time you asked me. I'm still sure."

"I've only asked—"

"Five times," Tabitha cut in. "Not that I'm counting or anything."

"I just wanted to make certain. It's easy to get turned around in areas like this."

"Like what?" August asked. "A nice neighborhood?"

"There are a lot of roads," she said, and Tabitha smirked.

"Right. Roads."

"All I'm saying is that it would be a shame to be late. The caseworker already told Jubilee that we'd be there."

Neither of her siblings responded.

Probably because they'd already discussed things. Malone had sent Quinn the address as soon as he'd returned home, and Quinn and Tabitha had programed it into the GPS system in Quinn's new Jeep. Seemed like a pretty fool-proof method. It also seemed pretty silly that Quinn was worried about finding the way.

She was worried about way more than that, though.

Malone had asked three times if she wanted him to fly up to Maine and drive back with her.

Three times, she'd said no.

Which seemed silly.

The fact was, she missed him.

The other fact was, she wondered if what she'd felt for him had just been a product of stress, fear, adrenaline. Had she conjured up feelings out of the depth of her desperation? Was it really possible that God was giving her a second shot at forever? That He'd brought a wonderful man into Quinn's life at the perfect time for her to be open to a new relationship?

Or was this just something Quinn had reached for because she was lonely, tired, ready for something different than the everyday workload she'd been carrying for so long?

"Stop worrying," Tabitha said, patting her shoulder. "It's going to be fine."

"You don't know that."

"Yeah. I do. He's a keeper."

"You know this because?" Quinn asked.

Tabitha touched the back of her head, wincing as she ran her fingers over the stitches that were hidden by her hair. "Getting my head bashed in gave me special powers."

"Powers to be annoying?" August asked, and Tabitha grinned.

"That, too. Anyway, you need to stop fretting, Quinn. You're making me nervous."

"Are you sure you're not nervous because

you're seeing Jubilee?" Quinn asked, and Tabitha shrugged, her eyes deeply shadowed. She hadn't been sleeping well. Quinn had heard her pacing the floor in the guest bedroom every night since she'd been released from the hospital.

"It's been a week since I dropped her off with you, and she probably thinks I abandoned her. Just like everyone else in her life has."

"Now who's the one worrying?" August asked gently. "She's a little kid, Tabitha, and you've mothered her for three years. She's not going to hate you because you were apart for a couple of days."

August had stayed in Echo Lake to help Quinn find a new vehicle and clean up her house. That's what he'd said, but there seemed to be something more to his presence. He'd been a lot kinder to Tabitha, a lot more willing to offer her the benefit of the doubt since she'd been out of the hospital.

As a result, Tabitha was more relaxed, more herself. Which had made the trip to Maryland easier than Quinn had anticipated. Good thing, since she really was a nervous wreck.

"She may hate me because I'm not going to be her mother anymore." Tabitha cleared her throat, brushed a lock of hair off her cheek. "Which is fine. I'm totally cool with that."

"No," Quinn said. "You're not. It would hurt a lot if that happened. Why not just admit it?"

"Why not just go back to discussing you and your boyfriend? I find that to be a lot more fun."

"Of course you do," Quinn murmured.

"Because it's way more exciting than talking about my new job at Betty Sue's Diner. I seriously can't believe I'm going to be living in my sister's apartment and working as a waitress."

"It's better than being dead," August pointed out.

"You're right about that. But, even better than that would be a boyfriend who sent me flowers every day. That's what Malone has done, right?"

She knew he had, so Quinn ignored the question.

"Nice flowers, too. Not the cheap kind most men like to give," Tabitha continued, the anxiety still in her eyes.

"They'd better be nice," August added. "If they weren't, he and I would have to have a talk."

"You're not going to talk to him about anything, August."

"Says who?"

"Says me."

"Sorry, sis. You've got no control over what I say or don't." He pulled into the driveway of a pretty little bungalow. Flower baskets hung from the porch eaves and a tire swing swayed gently from the branch of a giant oak tree. Three cars were parked in the driveway, and August pulled up behind a dark sedan.

He parked the Jeep and jumped out, stretching for a moment before leaning back into the vehicle. "Are you two going to sit there all day?" he asked, when neither Quinn nor Tabitha moved.

"You first," Tabitha said nervously, gesturing for Quinn to get out.

Quinn figured she needed to set a good example, so she opened her door, smoothing her skirt again as she stepped into watery sunlight.

The front door opened, and a pretty young woman walked out, a baby in her arms and a cute little girl beside her.

"Hello!" she called. "You must be Jubilee's other family. I'm Scout Anderson. This little girl," she said, setting her hand on the child's head, "is our daughter Lucy, and the baby is Ainslie."

"Nice to meet you," August said, striding forward with his hand outstretched.

Quinn followed, telling the butterflies in her stomach to settle down. No need to get so excited. Especially when she hadn't even seen Malone yet.

It was possible he hadn't arrived, possible that he wouldn't be able to come. He had a busy schedule, an active life. He'd told her he had a mission scheduled for the following week.

No way could he just drop everything—

The door opened again and Malone stepped out. Chance followed, with a very tall, very muscular redhead right behind him.

Boone Anderson.

It had to be. The eyes were just like Jubilee's.

Tabitha must have noticed. She gasped, took a step back.

"You look just like her," she said, and the man smiled.

"Hopefully the poor kid doesn't look just like me. Boone Anderson. Kend— *Jubilee's* father." He offered his hand the same way his wife had, and Quinn took it by rote. Her eyes were on Malone, though—his dark gaze, the sharp angle of his jaw, the familiar tilt of his mouth when he smiled.

"Malone," she said, the name just kind of slipping out.

He didn't wait for an invitation, just crossed the distance between them and pulled her into his arms.

"You look beautiful," he whispered in her ear, and her cheeks heated at the compliment, the butterflies she'd been trying to control taking flight.

"So do you."

"I don't think that I've ever been told that before." He chuckled, his arm winding through hers as he walked her to the edge of the porch, letting Chance, Boone, Scout and Tabitha talk quietly among themselves.

"What I meant was—"

"You don't need to explain, Quinn," he said, all the humor falling away. "You're nervous. I can understand that."

"Aren't you?"

He studied her for a moment, his beautiful dark gaze skimming over her face, dropping to the soft white sweater she'd bought to go with the skirt, settling on the hair she'd curled to within an inch of its life.

That had been hours ago.

It was probably limp and ratty now.

But when Malone looked at her? It felt perfect.

Finally, he touched her cheek, resting his palm against her skin. "I'm not nervous for anyone but you. You've been through a lot, you've lost a lot. I don't want to rush you. I don't want to make you let go of something you're not ready to release."

He lifted her right hand, touching the gold band she still wore. "I guess what I'm saying is, we can take our time. All those flowers I sent you—"

"Were beautiful."

"Boone said they might be overkill."

"What does Boone know?" she asked, and he laughed.

"That's what his wife said, but then I started thinking that you might feel overwhelmed, and I thought—"

"You *are* nervous."

"Because I don't want to hurt you without meaning to, bring up old feelings that you're not ready to face," he admitted, and for the first time since she'd met him, he looked vulnerable and a little unsure.

"I loved Cory with my whole heart. I didn't think there'd ever be room for someone else. Then I met you, and I realized…" She shook her head, the words so hard to come by, the feelings so difficult to express. "You fit here, Malone." She touched her chest. "In a way I never expected."

"I'm glad to hear that," he said, pulling her into his arms. "Because you're the person I didn't know I was missing, the piece to the puzzle I didn't know I was looking for. You fit. Not just in my heart. In my life. I don't want to mess it up."

"I don't think you could, Malone," she said honestly. "We just kind of…work together. And it's nice. Better than nice."

"That's good to know, because I ordered flowers to be delivered for the entire two weeks I'll be gone on my next mission. I was trying to figure out a way to cancel them. I guess now, I won't have to." He grinned, and she felt her heart melt just a little more for him.

"Two weeks is a long time. I'll miss you."

"I'll miss you, too, but I'll be back. Probably with more flowers in hand. I'm not all that creative when it comes to this kind of stuff."

That made her laugh.

She was still laughing when he leaned in for a kiss. Sweet and light and undemanding.

She reached up, her cast bumping his shoulder as she pulled him closer.

"Hey, lovebirds!" August called from beneath the old oak. Somehow he had ended up with the little girl named Lucy. She climbed onto the swing, and was shouting for him to push her.

"Jubilee is here." He gestured to a small SUV that was puttering up the road. It pulled into the driveway, idled there for a moment.

Suddenly, the sweet moment was gone, the peaceful afternoon was filled with tension. Lucy scrambled off the swing and ran to her mother, clutching her hand as the driver's door opened and Jubilee's caseworker stepped out.

She smiled, offered a quick wave and walked to the back of the car.

Boone stood in the watery sunlight, his hair burnished fire, his face filled with longing and hope and fear.

Jubilee's father, but the little girl didn't know it.

She got out of the car slowly, her scrawny legs appearing first—bruised and battered from whatever games she'd been playing outdoors. Then her head, her long hair the same deep red as her father's.

She hesitated there, not taking the hand the caseworker offered, just surveying the people waiting for her. Quinn tried to imagine it from her perspective. Seeing the woman holding the baby, tears glistening on her face. The tall man who looked as if he didn't know if he should move forward or step back. The guy under the tree, pushing the empty swing.

The little girl who smiled shyly.

Tabitha.

Quinn knew the moment Jubilee spotted her. Her face lit up, the hesitation fading.

"Mommy?" she said, exiting the car, waiting to be called forward.

Tabitha glanced at Boone and he nodded, stepping aside so she could move past. Run past. She nearly flew, rushing to Jubilee and lifting her into her arms.

"Ju-bee, I've missed you!" she cried.

No response, but Jubilee clung to her, whispered something in her ear.

"He's...gone," Tabitha said. "You don't have to see him again. But, there's somebody else I want you to meet. A few people, really." Her voice cracked but she put Jubilee down, turned her so she was facing Boone. "Remember that story I told you a long time ago? The one about the princess who got taken from her father and had to live with a horrible ogre?"

Jubilee nodded, staring up at Boone with wide-eyed fascination. It must have been strange to see someone with her hair color, her skin tone, her eyes.

"Remember how her father, the king, was searching everywhere for years and years, and finally one day he found her and brought her home? Well, you're kind of like that princess, Ju-bee, and this man? He's like the king. He's your real father, and he's been looking for you for a long time. And that lady there?" She pointed to Scout. "She's going to be—"

"I'm Scout," she interrupted, her voice gentle, her expression sweet and understanding, the tears still slipping down her face. "Your father's wife. You can call me Scout for now, if you want. Maybe in a few months you'll want to call me something else and that will be okay, too."

"A stepmother," Jubilee gasped, that quick

brain that Quinn had seen just a glimpse of making the connection.

"A good one," Tabitha rushed to say. "A really good one. With two sweet little girls who are going to be your sisters."

"But…what about you?" Jubilee clutched Tabitha's hand, her lower lip trembling.

"She's going to be with me, and she'll call and come visit you all the time," Quinn said, Malone's hand warm on her shoulder. It felt good to do this with him, to be part of what he and his team had been working toward for years. It felt even better to know that Jubilee would be okay now. Jarrod was in jail. The police had found the blood-splattered clothes in a small chest in the attic where Tabitha had hidden them. He'd been arrested for murder, assault, money laundering.

"You'll take care of her?" Jubilee said, looking straight into Quinn's eyes, asking her to make promises again.

This time, Quinn knew she could keep them.

Tabitha had changed. Loving Jubilee had done that to her.

"I will."

"Promise?"

"I promise," Quinn said.

Chance stepped off the porch, gave Boone

a gentle nudge. "You're giant-size. You might want to get down on her level," he suggested.

And Boone crouched, reaching into his jacket pocket, and pulling something from it. A tiny rosebud, pink and soft.

"This is for you, Jubilee. It reminds me of when you were a baby. You had a pretty little rosebud mouth and bright red hair. You were the prettiest baby I'd ever seen."

He held the flower out, and Jubilee took it, tucked it into the pocket of her jeans. She didn't offer a smile, didn't say a word. Just took Boone's hand and walked over to Lucy. The two little girls stared at each other for several long moments, and then Lucy smiled.

"Let's swing. You like to swing, right, Ju-bee? That man is going to push us."

She pointed at August, who gave a belabored sigh, a hint of a smile in his eyes.

And then the girls were racing to the swing. Apart and then suddenly together, holding hands as they reached August. He helped them onto the tire, cautioned them to hold on as Lucy begged to be pushed higher and higher.

"It's going to be okay," Boone said to no one in particular, his gaze on his daughters. "God has done this thing for us. He's in control of it. In His time, it will be what it should be. For now, let's just be thankful for what we have."

That was it, the spell was broken.

The adults began to mill around, talking and chatting about kids and work and weather. The caseworker suddenly had the baby in her arms, and Scout was serving tall glasses of lemonade.

Despite the awkwardness, the newness, it was a family. Not just parents and kids, but friends, all working together for a common goal. To make the transition as easy as it could be, to maintain old relationships, to build new ones.

"What are you thinking?" Malone asked, brushing a strand of hair from Quinn's cheek and looking into her eyes. "Because, whatever it is, it's making you smile."

"Just thinking you're not the only one who gives flowers. That was sweet, what Boone did."

"He loves her. Flowers are a small token of that."

"You know what else I was thinking?" she asked, studying his handsome face, his dark eyes and that scar that told the story about the kind of man he was. One who would sacrifice everything for the people he loved, who'd give his life for those he cared about.

"What?" he asked with a gentle smile.

"That this is a small token, too." She slipped the ring from her finger, slid it onto his pinky. "Take it with you when you go, Malone."

"Are you sure?" he asked, and she nodded, her throat tight with tears of sorrow and of joy.

He nodded, leaning in, his lips brushing hers.

"I love you, Quinn," he whispered. "More than the ocean loves the shore."

"I love you, too," she responded, and he kissed her again. With hope. With love. With promises for the moment and for the future.

"Hey, lovebirds!" August called. "Break it up! The kiddos are watching."

"That brother of yours is becoming a pest," Malone muttered.

And Quinn laughed, the sound ringing out into the afternoon, floating on wings of joy into the beautiful summer sky.

* * * * *

Dear Reader,

Quinn Robertson knows what it's like to walk the path of sorrow and despair. After losing her husband to brain cancer, she struggles to see the goodness of God through the difficulties she faces. Her journey is one we all must take. None of us is untouched by difficulties, and as I wrote Quinn's story, I couldn't help thinking about how much greater God is than the temporary challenges life brings our way. It isn't just an attitude of acceptance that gets us through these difficult times, but a deep-seated understanding that in the darkest moments, we are not alone.

May you find peace through Him today!

I love hearing from readers. You can drop me a line at shirlee@shirleemccoy.com or connect with me on Facebook or Twitter!

Shirlee McCoy

LARGER-PRINT BOOKS!

GET 2 FREE
LARGER-PRINT NOVELS
PLUS 2 FREE
MYSTERY GIFTS

Love Inspired®

Larger-print novels are now available...

YES! Please send me 2 FREE LARGER-PRINT Love Inspired® novels and my 2 FREE mystery gifts (gifts are worth about $10). After receiving them, if I don't wish to receive any more books, I can return the shipping statement marked "cancel." If I don't cancel, I will receive 6 brand-new novels every month and be billed just $5.49 per book in the U.S. or $5.99 per book in Canada. That's a savings of at least 19% off the cover price. It's quite a bargain! Shipping and handling is just 50¢ per book in the U.S. and 75¢ per book in Canada.* I understand that accepting the 2 free books and gifts places me under no obligation to buy anything. I can always return a shipment and cancel at any time. Even if I never buy another book, the two free books and gifts are mine to keep forever.

122/322 IDN GH6D

Name _____ (PLEASE PRINT)

Address _____ Apt. #

City _____ State/Prov. _____ Zip/Postal Code

Signature (if under 18, a parent or guardian must sign)

Mail to the **Reader Service:**
IN U.S.A.: P.O. Box 1867, Buffalo, NY 14240-1867
IN CANADA: P.O. Box 609, Fort Erie, Ontario L2A 5X3

**Are you a current subscriber to Love Inspired® books
and want to receive the larger-print edition?
Call 1-800-873-8635 or visit www.ReaderService.com.**

* Terms and prices subject to change without notice. Prices do not include applicable taxes. Sales tax applicable in N.Y. Canadian residents will be charged applicable taxes. Offer not valid in Quebec. This offer is limited to one order per household. Not valid to current subscribers to Love Inspired Larger-Print books. All orders subject to credit approval. Credit or debit balances in a customer's account(s) may be offset by any other outstanding balance owed by or to the customer. Please allow 4 to 6 weeks for delivery. Offer available while quantities last.

Your Privacy—The Reader Service is committed to protecting your privacy. Our Privacy Policy is available online at www.ReaderService.com or upon request from the Reader Service.

We make a portion of our mailing list available to reputable third parties that offer products we believe may interest you. If you prefer that we not exchange your name with third parties, or if you wish to clarify or modify your communication preferences, please visit us at www.ReaderService.com/consumerschoice or write to us at Reader Service Preference Service, P.O. Box 9062, Buffalo, NY 14240-9062. Include your complete name and address.